"There are different kinds of magic..."

Robert paused deliberately, and Aubrey prompted, "Such as?"

"The magic of a spring morning or a newborn baby," he said softly. "The magic of what happens between a man and a woman when they touch."

Slowly Robert drew her close, and Aubrey felt herself melting in his arms. He brushed her lips once, twice, then a third time with his own—until she was shivering and lifting her face to his, seeking deeper kisses. Until their bodies were molded together.

"Yes," she finally murmured. "Pure magic..."

Cara McLean shares her heroine's whimsical love of fairy tales and magical objects. She rereads *Peter Pan* and *The Little Prince* annually, and she's been building her unicorn collection since she was a child. This is Cara's first Temptation, one that definitely features a "perfect mix" of fantasy and earthy sensuality. Cara lives in Manhattan in a spacious apartment very similar to Aubrey's.

The Perfect Mix

CARA McLEAN

Harlequin Books

TORONTO • NEW YORK • LONDON
AMSTERDAM • PARIS • SYDNEY • HAMBURG
STOCKHOLM • ATHENS • TOKYO • MILAN

To Chuck, Martha, Brent, Jim,
Kathy and Nathan—with love

Published November 1986

ISBN 0-373-25231-5

Printed in Canada

1

THE THREE TEENAGE BOYS showed no signs of getting into their car and leaving. One would occasionally glance in Aubrey's direction, but for the most part they were content to lean against their car, drink their sodas and talk. Except for her car and theirs, there were only two others in the parking lot. Through the large windows of the all-night restaurant, she could see an older couple eating. The occupant of the fourth car was probably in the bathroom. Which left the three boys, Aubrey Jones and Aubrey's cat, Merlin, a purebred blue point Himalayan worth three hundred dollars.

Aubrey looked again at the boys, then down at Merlin, who was sitting quite naturally in the passenger seat. He returned Aubrey's stare as if to say, "Why are you just sitting there? Go get your coffee."

Aubrey sighed. "I've lived in New York too long," she said to the cat. "I'm sure those guys wouldn't try to steal you, but I really don't—"

She broke off when a car pulled in at her right and stopped abruptly. Before Aubrey could get a good look at the driver, he was out of the car and striding up the walk to the restaurant.

Not bothering to think about what she was doing, relying on instinct more than sense, Aubrey rolled down her window and stuck her head out. "Excuse me, sir!" she called. "Sir? Excuse me!"

Out of the corner of her eye, she could see the three boys staring at her, but she ignored them. She was watching the man, watching as he halted, stayed motionless for a moment, then slowly turned. He gave her plenty of time to notice that he had thick brown hair that shone with rusty highlights, that his shoulders filled his beige windbreaker quite well, that his not new yet not very faded jeans fit nicely across his backside and thighs.

"Uh-oh," she muttered as the man completed his turn, spotted her and started moving toward her. "I don't think this was such a good idea."

He walked slowly, and she noted that his jeans fit as well in the front as they did in the back, that underneath his jacket was a lightweight sweater that pulled across a taut belly as he moved and that he was disconcertingly attractive.

But no, she corrected herself quickly, his looks weren't that special. She was just, unfortunately, a sucker for a strong chin and jaw, for lips so thinly drawn that the mouth could look grim, yet so beautifully shaped that the smile was breathtaking, for a straight, almost aristocratic nose that would look fabulous in profile. Her only disappointment, as he bent down to bring his face to her level, was that it was too dim for her to see the color of his eyes.

"Were you calling me?" he asked.

Aubrey blinked. It scarcely seemed fair that such a wonderful example of male beauty should also have a fabulous voice. "Uh, yes," she said, finding her own voice after an embarrassing pause. "I was wondering if you could do me a favor."

He cocked his head to one side and raised a brow as if to say, "Yes?"

"Well, you see," she went on, "maybe I've lived in New York too long, but I really don't want to leave Merlin in the car with those boys just hanging around, and I certainly can't take him in."

The man looked over his shoulder at the boys, who were still looking Aubrey's way, then turned back and said, "Merlin?"

Hearing his name from a stranger, Merlin immediately popped up to check out what was happening. Raising his magnificent tail to full mast, he delicately stepped onto his mistress's lap and lifted an adorable, inquisitive face to the man at the window, his little nose twitching.

"Ah, Merlin," the man said, and held up a hand for him to sniff.

As Merlin was happily investigating his hand, the man turned his attention back to Aubrey. "I see your problem," he said. "What can I get you?"

"Oh, thank you," Aubrey said, dislodging Merlin slightly—who had done with sniffing the man's hand and was now butting it, asking to be petted—as she reached into her blazer pocket for some money. "Two large coffees," she said, handing the man two dollars. "One black, one regular, no sugar."

"That's it?"

"Well . . ." She grimaced as Merlin, in his excitement to get closer to the man, who had begun petting him, set a hind foot directly on Aubrey's bladder. "Uh, yes, that's it."

"Okay," the man said. He took a final swipe at Merlin's nose and left.

Aubrey watched him walk away, again admiring the fit of those jeans. "Nice man," she murmured to her cat, who was begging for more attention. "Must think I'm a little weird, though."

She rolled up the window and absently continued to pet Merlin while watching the man place his order at the take-out counter. Then he walked through the restaurant and disappeared in the direction of the rest rooms.

"Oh, lucky man," she said, lifting Merlin off her as the cat again tromped on her bladder. She shifted in the seat, trying to straighten her jacket and smooth her jeans. Realizing, rather dim-wittedly, she thought, that she could at least get out of the car and stand beside it, she did so. The night air was brisk, yet with a definite feel of spring to it, and she inhaled deeply. The boys, she noted, were watching, but she ignored them and stretched her arms high above her head until she heard some popping sounds. Then she brushed a few crumbs and stray cat hairs off her jeans and readjusted the silky knit scarf beneath the collar of her jacket. Feeling better for at least having moved, she was about to step back into her car when she saw her rescuer.

He was striding jauntily down the walk, a bright orange bag in one hand. He was taller, Aubrey realized as he neared her, than she had first thought. She herself stood over five eight in her sneakers, but he must easily top six feet in his.

"I got your coffees," he said when he reached her. "One black and one regular." He set the bag down on the hood of the car, then leaned against the car, his arms folded across his chest. With the light behind him, he was more a silhouette than a solid person, and she still couldn't tell the color of his eyes. She could tell, however, that those eyes were cataloging every inch of her.

She was wondering if she should be offended and just grab her coffees and leave when he spoke again.

"I was thinking," he said in his deep, rich voice, "especially since you plan on drinking two coffees, that you might need to use the rest room."

"Well, yes, I do," she said warily.

"If you think you can trust me, I'll stay here with your cat while you go inside."

Her entire body thought it was an excellent idea, but her mind put up a token protest. "I really can't ask you—" she began, but he interrupted her with a wave of a hand.

"I want to drink my own coffee and eat my sandwich before I start driving again anyhow. I can just as easily do it at your car as my own."

Very reasonable, she thought, turning her head slightly to catch a glimpse of the boys, one of whom was leaning against the car, facing her, staring rather insolently.

"Fine," she said suddenly. "If you'd prefer to sit down, you're welcome to my car. Just push Merlin aside." She started past him, then stopped and added, "Thanks a lot."

"No problem, ' he said.

She hurried up the walk, trying not to break into a run. Inside the restaurant, she didn't hesitate on her way to the rest rooms, thankful that at this time of night there'd be no line.

When she had disappeared inside the rest room, her rescuer climbed into her car. He sat down in the passenger seat, firmly telling Merlin to stay in the driver's seat. He took out his sandwich and coffee and as he began to eat, he examined the car.

It was several years old, but in good condition and neat. In the back seat were only a small suitcase, a canvas bag and a covered litter box, so he assumed the woman had been on a weekend trip, like him. He had been puzzled by her New Mexico plates, since she had said she lived in New York, but figured she was originally from the southwest and had never changed her registration. Considering the cost of owning and maintaining a car in New York, he couldn't blame her. His own car was rented.

As he sipped his coffee, he wondered where the woman could have gone for the weekend. Not many people would take a trip north during April, a muddy, wet month along the northern east coast. He smiled, realizing his curiosity about the woman was getting the better of him. She was a complete stranger. An attractive one, but a stranger nonetheless, and probably someone he'd never see again. They might both live in New York City, but it was a big city. And he had only done the woman a small favor, nothing that she would be eternally grateful for.

Still, he recalled the mesmerizing effect of her large dark eyes, the intriguing way her lithe body had moved when she'd stretched her arms above her head. He wondered how her hair, long and dark and pulled back into a ponytail, would feel. Her clothes were casual— jeans, a striped cotton shirt and a blazer—yet he found something charming about the eye-catching turquoise scarf around her neck. And he had rather liked playing Sir Galahad for her, although he'd never considered himself the knight-in-shining-armor type. He looked up when he glimpsed the restaurant door opening, and watched as his fair damsel in distress skipped down the steps, then strolled along the walk with an easy, long-legged stride. Maybe, he thought, he wouldn't have to lose touch with her when they pulled out of the parking lot. There had to be a way....

When Aubrey returned to her car, she found the man sitting in the passenger seat, popping the last bite of his sandwich into his mouth. Merlin was avidly watching every move he made, obviously certain the man had been provided for his amusement.

"Could you hold on to Merlin while I open the door?" Aubrey called through the closed window.

The man nodded, set down his coffee and pulled the cat onto his lap. Aubrey opened the door and slipped into her seat, mentally grimacing at the thought of all the cat hairs the back of her jeans and blazer were going to pick up.

"Have a nice time?" the man asked, handing her two coffees.

"Fabulous," she said. "Everyone should use a public rest room at least once a week. Makes you appreciate the finer things in life that much more."

The man chuckled, then asked, "Why two coffees?" as she took the lid off the black coffee and swallowed a large gulp of it.

"One for now, for a quick bolt of caffeine, and one for the rest of the trip to make sure I make it."

"And you like the taste of coffee with milk better than just black."

She nodded.

As she quickly gulped down her coffee and the man sipped his, silence filled the car, broken only by Merlin's loud, erratic purring. At first Aubrey concentrated on her coffee, but slowly she became aware of how small her economy car really was; of how the man had pushed the passenger seat all the way back to accommodate his long legs, of how his after-shave had faintly scented the air, of how large the hand holding the coffee cup was. And he was scrutinizing her, too.

She tossed back the rest of her coffee and cleared her throat. "So," she said brightly, "which way you headed?"

"Same as you, I would guess," he said, turning toward her. "New York."

"City?" she asked, sorry it was even darker in her car and therefore that much less likely that she could see the color of his eyes.

He nodded. "You live in Manhattan?"

"Upper West Side. And you?"

"Upper East Side," he said promptly, chuckling.

Aubrey smiled back. New York City, like any large city, she supposed, wasn't so much one huge metropolis as it was a collection of neighborhoods, each unique with its differing mixtures of residents, businesses, retail stores. There was artistic SoHo; the trendy, expensive, open-seven-days-a-week Village; quiet Chelsea; bustling midtown, where most of the city's corporate offices were, along with Saks Fifth Avenue, Tiffany's, the Twenty-One Club. There was the older but recently revitalized Upper West Side, its residents ranging from elderly people who had lived there for years and years, to jazz musicians and opera singers, any of whom could be found on a given Saturday strolling along Broadway, that still slightly seedy and always wide-awake lifeline of the city. And there was the Upper East Side, with street after street of charming brownstones and town houses, its multitude of ritzy doctors' offices and a populace that seemed, at least to Aubrey, to be made up almost entirely of young corporate professionals. Staring at her attractive companion, she wondered if he fit into his neighborhood as well as she fit into hers.

"Shall we argue," she said, "about the merits of our respective neighborhoods, like good New Yorkers?"

He shook his head. "I never argue with someone when I don't know her name."

"Oh, that's right. I'm Aubrey Jones." She held out her hand.

He took it in a firm grip. Despite the dimness in the car, she thought she saw a faint gleam in his eye. "And I'm Robert Browning," he said.

The way he said it, he might have been joking, but Aubrey instantly knew he was testing her. Figuring without difficulty how most people would respond to his name— "As in Barrett? As in 'How do I love thee . . . '?" or something equally mundane— Aubrey shook his hand and grinned.

"'She had,'" she said, "'a heart . . . too soon made glad, too easily impressed.'" She watched with satisfaction as his eyes widened and a smile played at one corner of his mouth.

"Very good," he murmured. He gave her hand a final squeeze, then let go. "'My Last Duchess.' Few people know any of Browning's poetry, only that he was married to Elizabeth Barrett and that she wrote *Sonnets from the Portuguese*."

"I just always liked the Victorian period," Aubrey said, shrugging, sorry he had let go of her hand so quickly. "I don't suppose you're any relation."

"No. Actually, I was named for my mother's father. He was a Robert, and my father was a Browning. An unfortunate coincidence."

"Unfortunate? Why? It's a nice-sounding name. Robert Browning," she repeated thoughtfully. "Yes, I like the sound of it."

"Only because all your life you haven't had people making remarkably unimaginative comments about it when they meet you."

"Oh, yeah? Maybe not, but when I was in high school there was a song called 'Aubrey,' and believe me, I had that thing quoted at me so often I could sing it in my sleep."

"'Aubrey' . . ." he said musingly. "Didn't Bread do that song?"

She looked at him in surprise. "Yes. Don't tell me you know it."

"I don't remember it very well. It was a love song, wasn't it? He'd fallen in love with a girl named Aubrey and had lost her."

"Right. And he'd do most anything, even travel around the world a thousand times, just to be close to her again."

"And there was something about her name, that it was such an unusual name." Robert turned to Aubrey, and his piercing gaze made her catch her breath. "And such an unusual girl."

She gulped down some more coffee. This conversation was becoming a bit too personal. "And here you said you didn't remember the song that well. So tell me," she added brightly, "do people call you Bob or Rob or—"

"Robert."

She just caught herself from nodding sagely. She was honest enough to admit that she judged people too quickly, which was exactly what she was tempted to do with Robert Browning. He didn't appear to appreciate the eccentric humor of being named after a famous person, he lived on the Upper East Side, he preferred to be called Robert and his windbreaker sported a London Fog label. And he was attractive and wore wonderful after-shave and had warm, comforting hands and an intriguing half smile . . . and was again staring at her as keenly as she was staring at him.

Aubrey blinked. He was still staring at her and seemed to have moved closer, though that couldn't be possible. His eyes were still shadowed, yet she felt their intensity, knew when he was concentrating on her own eyes, then her mouth, then her throat. She swallowed, unable to command her body to do any more, uncertain she even wanted to move again. That little action seemed to bestir Robert, though, for his gaze shifted back to her eyes, and he cleared his throat.

"Where exactly do you live on the Upper West Side?" he asked.

She could move again, his voice having released her, and she made a little business of stuffing her empty coffee cup into a plastic trash bag and taking the lid off her second cup as she answered. "Ninety-third and Riverside."

"In one of those big old buildings?"

She nodded and sipped her coffee. "And in one of those big old apartments."

"And you probably pay half as much rent as I do for my very small apartment."

She grinned, glad the normal conversation had obliterated the earlier intensity. "Probably."

"You know," he went on, idly stroking the sleeping Merlin, "I'm not so much a hidebound East Sider as you may think."

She raised her brows skeptically. "Oh?"

"Not at all. As a matter of fact, one of my favorite places to eat is a restaurant on the West Side. Alex's."

Aubrey choked as the coffee slid down the wrong way. Robert immediately began hitting her on the back as she coughed and spluttered. She swallowed several more gulps of the cool coffee to clear her windpipe, and finally the coughing stopped.

"All right?" he asked, close to her ear.

She nodded and wiped her eyes with the back of one hand.

"You sure?" he persisted.

She nodded again, although she really wasn't. How could she be when Robert was leaning lightly against her, his warm hand still pressed against her back, his breath wafting across her flushed cheek? She shifted slightly, whether to move away or closer to him she wasn't sure, but it didn't matter. He instantly moved back, absently soothing the disturbed cat.

"Phew," she said after taking a deep breath. "That was unexpected."

"I hope it wasn't anything I said," he joked.

"Uh, actually, I think it was. I was surprised when you said you go to Alex's. I thought that was one of the West Side's best kept secrets."

"You can't keep great food at those prices secret for very long. I take it you go there yourself."

"Oh, yes." Aubrey tentatively sipped her coffee and mentally crossed her fingers. "I'm a regular there. Almost every Saturday night."

"Really? I don't remember ever seeing you there."

"Well, I'm usually at the bar. I don't generally go for dinner. Besides," she added teasingly, glancing at him from the corner of her eye, "I'm sure you don't go there alone and don't spend your time checking out other women."

He chuckled. "True. But—" his voice somehow grew lower and dangerously familiar "—I have a feeling you'd be hard to miss, no matter where you were or who I was with."

He began to toy with her scarf, as though almost touching her like that, his fingers so close to her breast, was the most natural thing in the world. Aubrey stopped breathing, afraid that if she did breathe, he *would* touch her. And what would be wrong with that, she asked herself. Even as she tried to come up with an answer, he dropped his hand and moved slightly away.

"Sorry," he mumbled. "I didn't mean to make you uncomfortable."

She quickly turned to him. "No," she said, her voice a little breathless, "you didn't make me uncomfortable. You just surprised me."

That little half smile played at the corner of his mouth again. "That makes two of us," he said, then nonchalantly glanced at his watch. "Damn, I didn't realize it was that late. We're not going to get to New York till after midnight."

"I suppose we should get going," she said slowly. She was enjoying this brief interlude but knew it should go no further. She firmly told herself Robert Browning wasn't her type, but refused to examine the reasoning behind that belief.

"Pity we can't ditch one of the cars," he said. "It would save on gas."

She nodded, searching madly for something to say, not wanting another dangerous silence to descend on them, and, in some strange way, draw them closer.

A loud click interrupted her worrying, and she looked up to see that Robert had opened his door a crack, and that Merlin was eagerly trying to get out.

"Oh, here, let me take him." She lifted the cat and held him against her breast as Robert opened the door all the way. "Thank you," she added as he placed one leg out.

He turned back to her. "My pleasure. Really. He's a wonderful cat, and it would have been a shame if you'd lost him." He stroked Merlin's head, his fingers brushing once against Aubrey's chin. She almost gasped at the jolt that light touch sent through her, but stopped herself in time and merely tightened her hold on Merlin.

"Well, thank you again," she said inanely. "And drive safely."

"Which way are you going into the city?" he asked, dropping his hand and staring directly into her eyes.

She didn't answer. She couldn't. She was too busy looking at his eyes, now clearly revealed by the car's interior light. They were blue, a true, beautiful blue, as airy and clear as a cloudless spring day.

"Your eyes are blue," she murmured.

He cocked his head slightly, questioningly. "I know."

"I mean, they're pure blue, no other color in them. You must have a lot of recessive blue-eye genes in your family."

He neither said nor did anything for a moment. He just stared, his mouth a straight line. Then he smiled, a full, glorious smile. "You are a most intriguing woman, Aubrey Jones," he said. "I'll be your Sir Galahad anytime."

He didn't wait for her answer, but slid out of the car, locked the door then pushed it shut. Without hesitation he turned and got into his own car and started the engine. He didn't pull away then; he just looked over at her. Moving automatically, Aubrey set Merlin down in the passenger seat, started her own car, shifted into reverse, then nodded to Robert. He backed out of his parking space and headed for the exit, Aubrey right behind him. As she drove, she noted absently that the parking lot was empty, the other three cars already gone. She hadn't noticed them leave.

AT THAT HOUR, even on a Sunday night, the traffic was light going into New York. Aubrey followed Robert for several miles, keeping a constant distance between them. Then slowly, slowly, she eased up on the accelerator, dropping from sixty-five to fifty-five and losing herself in a pack of slow-moving cars. When she could finally no longer discern Robert's taillights, she felt an easing of the tension in her shoulders and neck . . . and a vague sadness.

She wasn't averse to men or to being involved with them. Some of the best times of her life had included men. But never a man like Robert, with his obvious self-assurance, his maturity and whatever depths his pure blue eyes concealed. The men she dated were often more like boys, with their youthful cockiness, their passion for large parties in large lofts and dates that ended at dawn in all-night restaurants, their unwavering belief that just around any corner, magic was waiting for them, waiting to fly them away to better things. Her relationships with these men weren't serious; they were free of commitment and brief—for when the magic never appeared, the men moved on. But Robert, Aubrey knew instinctively, wasn't a boy one saw idly while he chased pipe dreams. Robert was a man, in all the varied and powerful meanings of the word. More a Sir Lancelot than the virginal Sir Galahad, and she was fairly certain she had no need of a knight in shining armor.

ROBERT WAS INSTANTLY AWARE of Aubrey's dropping back. He'd been looking often into his rearview mirror and had seen her headlights fading, slowly but surely. He could have slowed down himself, but she might have just speeded up and shot past him. No, he'd let her go this time, for he'd found a way to see her again. And he had to see her again. During that short time in her car, he'd lost himself in the beauty of her eyes, in the huskiness of her voice, become entranced by her graceful movements. He felt as though he'd relinquished a small piece of himself to Aubrey, and that should have scared him. Instead he found himself speeding up as he approached the New York City expressways, as if he could make next Saturday come sooner.

2

AT NINE O'CLOCK the following Saturday night, Robert walked into Alex's. The restaurant was long and narrow and divided by a wall into two separate rooms, the bar on the right, the dining room on the left. Since he always went to Alex's for dinner, Robert had never been in the bar before, and he was surprised by the number of people there. Every stool was taken; several people with drinks in their hands stood at a counter to the side. Perhaps the unusually mild late April evening had convinced everyone to start celebrating spring. Robert looked around the room, at the long wooden bar, the wooden stools covered in deep blue leather, at the light-colored walls and the multitude of posters, paintings and photographs of sunny Greece and its turquoise ocean.

Idly wondering how many of Alex's customers ended up visiting Greece at some point, Robert scanned the crowd, his gaze lingering on every dark-haired woman. He couldn't see Aubrey. Of course, he didn't know if she'd be there, of even if she might have been and gone by now. Sir Galahad in search of the Grail, he thought, then decided to walk the length of the bar to make sure Aubrey wasn't there.

She wasn't. He reached the far end without seeing her and was surprised by his strong feeling of disappointment. He scarcely knew the woman, he told himself. He might not even recognize her again.

That wasn't true. Robert knew he'd recognize her if they were on opposite sides of Broadway, if only because of the excitement that would fill him. The same excitement he'd felt when he'd first heard her calling to him, when he'd leaned down and looked into her dark eyes, when she'd sat beside him in her small car. When he'd almost kissed her.

Someone brushed against him, and Robert looked up, startled, not certain for a moment where he was. A woman, the person who had bumped into him, he presumed, smiled invitingly at him. When he simply stared back at her, sorry that her hair was red and not a lustrous black, she shrugged and turned to the bar.

Now what, he asked himself, stepping aside as a couple tried to get past him. Should he wait, hoping Aubrey would come later? Definitely. She was probably a late-night person and wouldn't arrive before ten. And she would arrive!

That decided, Robert eased his way to the bar and leaned against it, squeezing between two stools. An attractive woman in black on one of the stools glanced at him when he accidentally nudged her shoulder, smiled briefly, then turned back to her companion. Robert was just about to lean forward to catch the bartender's eye when the woman suddenly turned around again. He looked at her questioningly, and she grinned.

"Your eyes are pure blue," she said.

Robert blinked. To be told that twice in one week was a bit much. "Yes," he said slowly.

"Is your name Robert?"

He nodded. "Yes."

"I'm Maggie." The woman held out her hand, and he shook it, feeling more and more confused. "I'm Aubrey's roommate," she added.

His grip tightened for a moment, then he released her hand. "Aubrey's roommate?" he repeated. "Is she here?"

Maggie giggled. "Haven't found her yet, huh? Well, order a drink, and I'm sure you'll see her."

She winked and turned back to the man beside her.

"Now I know how Alice in Wonderland felt," Robert muttered under his breath. Still, he was pleased. He'd obviously made enough of an impact on Aubrey that she had told her roommate about him, right down to the blue eyes. And she was here. Smiling, he followed Maggie's instructions and leaned forward to get the bartender's attention, and felt his mouth drop open.

She was wearing a white cotton shirt with the sleeves rolled up to her elbows and tight black jeans. Around her neck was a scarf identical to the turquoise one, except this one was a dusty rose. She had wrapped it around her throat twice, and the ends dangled down her back. Her hair was in a ponytail again; it swung in unison with the scarf ends as she rapidly mixed a drink.

Aubrey was a bartender, Robert thought with amazement. The bartender at Alex's. He started to chuckle. No wonder she'd said she was a regular here. He glanced to his side and saw that Maggie was watching him.

"You found her," she said.

"Yep."

"You don't mind?"

"Why should I mind?" He leaned an elbow on the bar, turning sideways so that he could look at Maggie and still keep an eye on Aubrey. "And why didn't she just tell me?"

Maggie shrugged. "Why should she? You didn't ask her to meet you here for drinks or anything. I don't think she really expected you to show up."

He looked speculatively at Maggie. There was a defensiveness about her, but not for herself. It was for Aubrey. "I always heard," he said slowly, "that when a knight rescues a maiden in distress, he gets to keep her. I thought Aubrey understood that."

Maggie narrowed her eyes as she returned his stare. Then she smiled. "I've certainly heard of that custom, but I fear Aubrey's a little uneducated in such matters. She knows a lot about Merlin, but I don't think she knows much about knights. You'll have to instruct her."

Realizing he had an ally, though not sure why he needed one, Robert smiled that half smile that had so intrigued Aubrey. "I'll keep that in—"

"Can I get you a drink?" a man interrupted him.

Robert looked up to find Alex himself standing before him on the other side of the bar. "Hello, Alex," he said. "How's it goin'?"

"Hey, Robert." Alex smiled broadly. "You can see how it's going. I don't think it's ever been this busy before. How's it going for yourself? Haven't seen you around for a while."

Robert shrugged. "I've been doing all right."

"Glad to hear it. Now what can I get you?"

Robert nodded to the far end of the bar where Aubrey was. Obviously with such a crowd, she and Alex had split bar duty. "You can get me your other bartender."

Alex raised a thick dark brow. "Aubrey? You know her?"

"A little."

Alex laughed, a hearty, heavy sound. "That's about as well as any of us knows Aubrey, eh? All right, my friend. I'll switch places with her."

Robert watched as the large man strolled down the bar, stopping for a moment to greet a few customers, then laid a hand on Aubrey's shoulder. He saw her look up, frown, then glance down the bar. Robert raised a hand in greeting, then smiled to himself as Aubrey's eyes widened and guilt chased surprise across her face. She looked up at Alex, said something then walked down the bar.

He came, Aubrey thought, elation and trepidation busily fighting it out in her stomach. And apparently he didn't mind that she was a bartender, although he could just be being polite. But no, she thought as she was halted by a customer who asked for a whiskey sour, if he minded he would have just left. Or maybe—she scooped up some ice—he was meeting some friends here, had seen her and just wanted to say hello. Yes, that was it. He hadn't come specifically to see her, some strange woman he'd met in a parking lot a week earlier. She would simply say hi, fix him a drink, chat for a minute then go about her business. She hadn't really expected or wanted anything more when she'd contemplated his coming here, had she? Of course not. Then why did a mere glance from him make her breath catch in her throat, her stomach jump and her heart flutter?

She gave the customer his whiskey sour, made change from his five, pocketed her tip and continued down the bar. Robert was staring intently at her, his gaze roving over her face, her body. Although she always wore this outfit to work, she suddenly wondered if the shirt was too plain and unattractive, the pants indecently tight. Then she was standing in front of him and, despite her insistence that this was a casual meeting between practically strangers, she could think of nothing but how astonishingly blue his eyes were, how beautiful his mouth was when he smiled like that, how well he looked in a dark sports jacket and blue shirt. How much she wanted to touch him.

She shoved her hands in her pockets. "Hi," she said.

"Hi," he said.

"Uh, can I get you a drink?"

"Scotch on the rocks."

She nodded and quickly fixed the drink. She set it down in front of him, then shook her head when he reached for his wallet.

"It's on the house," she said.

He toasted her and took a sip of the drink. Maggie, who had been watching unabashedly, suddenly leaned forward.

"I've got to be going, P.T.," she said to Aubrey, although she winked at Robert. "See you back at the apartment." She slid off her stool. "Have a seat, Robert, and . . . I hope to see you again."

He smiled, nodded and said, "Same here," then quickly sat down before someone else could. When he looked up, Aubrey had moved down to the near end of the bar and was loading a black tray with drinks. She made half a dozen of them, which the waitress garnished herself with swizzle sticks and lemon, lime or cherry. Then Aubrey returned to Robert.

"It's kind of crowded in here tonight," she said.

"What do you expect," he said, "when someone who looks like you is tending bar?"

She looked at him curiously. "I think that was a compliment, so thank you."

"You look so shocked," he said, that little half smile teasing the corner of his mouth. "One would think you've never been complimented before."

"No, I...uh, well..." Damn, Aubrey thought. That's what she got for jumping to conclusions about people. Robert just hadn't struck her earlier as the compliment-giving type.

"Anyhow," she said, smiling brightly, "I'm afraid I don't have much time to talk. But...it sure is nice to see you again." Her voice was too loud, her words spoken too quickly, but she forgave herself. She was nervous. She wasn't sure why she was nervous. It might simply be because he was running a long finger around the lip of his glass in a surprisingly suggestive way, or because he was staring at her so intently, seeming to delve right into her soul while revealing none of his own.

"It's very nice to see you again, too, Aubrey," he said. "How long do you think this crowd will last?"

"It should start to thin by around eleven or twelve."

"And what time do you get off?"

She blinked. "Two," she whispered.

He leaned across the bar. "I didn't hear you. What did you say?"

She swallowed. Did he know how close his hand was to hers? Could he feel her warmth as well as she could feel his? "Two," she repeated. "I get off at two."

He drew a finger across her knuckles and sat back. "Fine," he said.

"Aubrey," a stern but quiet voice suddenly said, "you know I'm all for young love, think it's grand, but would you mind getting to work?"

"Oh, Alex." Aubrey turned to her boss, mortified at her negligence.

Alex grinned. "Don't worry about it. He is kind of a good-lookin' dude. Almost as good-lookin' as me."

She smiled weakly, then hurried down to the end of the bar, where a waiter had another drink order.

ALMOST THREE HOURS LATER, Robert was amazed at himself. He had never cared to sit in a bar before, especially alone, but he could think of few Saturday nights he'd enjoyed so much. He had chatted with some of the people sitting around him—Alex's attracted very interesting customers—and he'd been flattered by the subtle attention several women had paid him. But most of the time he'd concentrated on Aubrey, watched her fix drinks efficiently and with flair, chat easily with the customers. He'd felt twinges of unease when some of the younger men had flirted with her and been amazed at the sudden desire within him to announce to everyone there that Aubrey Jones was his lady.

That was ridiculous, he told himself. She wasn't; he scarcely knew her. And she certainly wasn't encouraging him. When she'd fixed him a second drink, she hadn't stopped to talk, and if their eyes happened to meet, she would look away quickly, not returning his smile. He would have been totally discouraged if he hadn't caught her staring at him once, her eyes wide and filled with speculation, hesitation and interest, one of her fingers rubbing across the knuckles he had caressed. When he'd smiled at her, she'd smiled, too, then seemed to snap back to awareness and hurriedly turned away. He had found her confusion endearing. If he had any doubts about pursuing this woman, they'd vanished then.

Now he glanced down the bar to where she was slipping glasses upside down into their holders above the counter. With her arms above her head, her shirt was pulled tight across her breasts, emphasizing their intriguing roundness. His gaze traveled downward to where the black jeans fit snugly across her belly and hips. The bar, unfortunately, impeded any lower investigation, so he focused on her head, on the lovely and thick black hair, on her high cheekbones, the almost too large nose that had character, the well-defined jaw and strong chin and the wonderfully long neck.

"Pretty good-lookin', isn't she?" Alex said, appearing on the other side of the bar from Robert.

Robert looked up and grinned. "You could always pick 'em, Alex."

Alex laughed. "But not like you can, my friend. Every time you come in here, you have some beautiful woman with you, hanging all over you.

"But tonight," he went on when Robert would have spoken, "you come in here alone, ask for my lady bartender to serve you and then stare at her all night. So tell me—" Alex leaned on the bar, confidentially close to Robert "—what do you know about our little Aubrey that we don't know? She's nervous that you stare so much, but the rest of us are delighted. She's too much a secret—and too alone."

Alex straightened and slapped Robert on the shoulder with a massive hand. "So you make sure she's not too much alone anymore, eh, Robbie?" He laughed and walked away, down toward Aubrey, leaving a rather puzzled Robert behind.

Had he just been warned, he wondered. Or had Alex simply been shooting the breeze? Robert was intrigued that Alex referred to Aubrey as a secret, for she seemed like a very open person. Obviously there were great depths to the woman. And he was pleased that Alex saw Aubrey as alone much of the time. Robert didn't want to have to bother convincing her to get rid of whatever man might be in her life. It would be a waste of time that could be put to much better use.

He saw that Alex was through talking with Aubrey and, with a little shove, the boss sent her in Robert's direction. He noticed her bemused expression and wondered if Alex had said something as confusing to her as he had to him.

"Well," she said when she stopped in front of him, "seems as if you carry more clout in this place than I thought."

He looked at her questioningly. "How's that?"

She sighed. "Alex just told me I could leave early tonight," she said flatly.

Robert tried unsuccessfully to bite back a smile. "In that case, I'd like to walk you home."

She looked at him for a long minute, and Robert could almost see the war being waged within her. Then she slowly nodded and said, "All right," and Robert felt he could see the far off gleam of the Grail.

AUBREY TOOK ONLY A FEW MINUTES to collect her things, brush out her hair and apply some lipstick. When she joined Robert at the bar and he slid off his stool, she was surprised to see that in her cowboy boots she could almost look him straight in the eye. Such inconsequential nonsense, she scolded herself as they walked to the door. But she knew that concentrating on such things as height would keep her from thinking about why she had been foolish enough to agree to this walk home. She'd seen the way Robert had looked at her all evening, knew that he hadn't hung around for three hours just because he hadn't anything better to do. She had also seen several different women approach him, signal him with looks that varied from timid to blatant. She hadn't been surprised; he was an attractive man, and there was about him an air of totally masculine assurance. His teasing half smile seemed to say, "I know who and what I am, who and what I want." And the gleam in his eye when he looked at Aubrey said, "I want you."

Despite herself she was intrigued, drawn to the gleam, the smile, the man, just as she had been almost a week earlier. She had stared at him covertly throughout the evening, and he'd only caught her at it once. That once, though, had been enough to remind her that she was playing with fire, that a man who had made as many conquests as this Sir Lancelot no doubt had wouldn't hesitate to stride into her bizarre yet comfortable life, reorder it to his taste, then stride back out. So why was she encouraging him? Aubrey shook her head. Temporary insanity, no doubt.

"You don't want to go home?" Robert asked, his voice breaking into her thoughts.

She suddenly realized he had spoken before and was interpreting her shake of the head as answer to his question. "No," she said, "that's not what I . . . I mean, yes, I'd like to go home now."

He smiled and brushed a lock of hair back from her face with a gentle finger. "Okay. Let's go."

They began walking up Columbus Avenue. There were, as always, people about, but only a few, and the street had a very quiet and sleepy feel to it. Rather like Main Street in a small town, Robert thought, suddenly wanting to take Aubrey's hand, as though he were a teenager walking his date home from the movie. But he wasn't, and it was enough for now that she was with him. The touching would come later.

"How long have you been a bartender?" he asked abruptly, pulling his mind back from the dangerous topic of touching.

"Oh, a little while," she answered evasively. "What do you do?"

"It's not nearly as exciting as bartending," he said, sending her a quick smile as they crossed Columbus. "I'm a lawyer, corporate law."

"Oh." She fought the inclination to add "corporate lawyer" to "Upper East Side" and "London Fog" and come up with a possibly erroneous result. Just because he was different from the pixie-dust-chasing free spirits she had dated before didn't mean he was a stuffy, staid lawyer. Stuffy, staid lawyers didn't sit in West Side bars for three hours. "I don't know anything about corporate law," she said. "Actually, I never wanted to be a lawyer," she added, almost to herself.

He chuckled. "You sound surprised that you didn't. Should you have wanted to be a lawyer?"

She laughed. She was feeling more comfortable with him now, perhaps because of the normal conversation, perhaps because he wasn't staring at her. "It seems I've wanted to be most everything else at one time or another. I think it was the thought of three years of law school that put me off."

"They are daunting, I'll— Watch out!" He grabbed her hand and pulled her to him as she stepped into the street, directly in front of a turning car.

The horn blew as the car sped past them. Robert didn't let go of Aubrey's hand and even put his other hand on her shoulder to steady her.

"Are you all right?" he asked anxiously. "I didn't mean to yank on you so hard."

"I'm okay," she said, and took a deep breath. "I didn't even see him."

"I don't think he really saw you, either, dressed all in black as you are."

She looked down at herself, at the black blazer she'd put on over her white shirt and at the black jeans. "My mother always told me to wear something light-colored at night." She looked up at Robert and was surprised to find concern lingering in his eyes.

"I'm all right," she said, placing a hand on his arm reassuringly. "Honest. And thank you for being a little more aware and quick-thinking than I."

He dropped his hand from her shoulder, and the worry left his face. He did not, however, release her hand. "We knights are supposed to be quick-thinking," he said lightly. He stroked her cheek, and she shivered slightly at his touch. "Besides," he added, his voice serious and deep, "I'd never want to see you hurt."

As had happened in her car, she felt paralyzed by his gaze and touch. For a long moment she simply stared up into his eyes, not knowing that, in the light from the street lamp directly above him, he could read in them her curiosity about him, the unadmitted attraction she felt toward him. He leaned forward and brushed his lips across hers, then pulled back, and the spell was broken.

Without speaking, they both turned uptown and continued walking, still holding hands. Aubrey liked the feel of Robert's hand. It was large yet fit comfortably into hers. It was also quite warm and had a few faint calluses on it. She wondered if they were from some sport like squash.

After walking a block in silence, they began talking again. Their conversation was light. Robert told her about growing up in a huge house in a small town in Connecticut with two younger sisters, a younger brother and three champion collies. Aubrey told him about working as a bartender, the crazy requests she sometimes got—she omitted the even crazier propositions—and the hilarious things some people could do when feeling relaxed and in friendly company at a bar. They both knew there was also a dark, sad side to some people who drank regularly in bars, but neither mentioned it.

When they reached the Riverside Drive entrance to her building, Robert gazed up at the mammoth structure with envy.

"I don't suppose there are any vacant apartments," he said wistfully.

She laughed as she unlocked the outside door. "You wouldn't really move from the East Side to the West, would you?"

He looked at her with some surprise. "Why not?"

Damn, Aubrey thought as she rang the bell for the doorman to unlock the inside door. She really had to watch herself. "Just teasing," she said over her shoulder as the doorman opened up.

"Good evening, Ms Jones," he said, shutting the door behind them.

"Hiya, Hal." She walked over to the elevator and pushed the Up button.

"Home early tonight, aren't you?" Hal asked, glancing at Robert.

"Uh-huh," she said. "Whoever said Alex has no heart was lying."

The elevator doors slid open, and Aubrey and Robert stepped inside.

"Have a nice night," Hal said, winking just as the doors closed.

"Dirty old man," Aubrey said cheerfully as the elevator began to climb to the eleventh floor. Robert didn't respond, and she turned to him.

That endearing half smile was on his lips again, and his eyes seemed to have grown even more blue from some inner fire. He moved slightly, subtly, closer to her, and she was reminded rather forcefully of how attractive this man was, of how well-built he was. And of how small and slow this elevator was.

"Does the alarm go off if you push the Stop button?" he asked, almost casually.

She swallowed, wondering why her mouth had suddenly gone dry. "What?" she asked faintly.

"Does the alarm go off if you push the Stop button?" he repeated, just as casually as before.

She shook her head, then watched with fascination as one of Robert's arms lifted, hand outstretched, and a long finger pushed the button. Immediately and without making a sound, the elevator stopped. For a moment neither of them moved or spoke; then Aubrey saw his hand move from the elevator panel toward her, the arm stretching across the distance between them, until his fingertips brushed her cheek.

"Aubrey," he whispered, and took a step closer.

His fingers slid into her thick hair, weaving through it. The hair itself seemed to tingle from the touch, then her scalp, all of her head, all of her body. He took a small step forward at the same time she did. Only inches remained between their bodies. His hand cupped the back of her head, tilting it upward to his. Slowly his head lowered, and Aubrey stared into his eyes, searching for something. Just before his lips touched hers she saw it, and closed her eyes.

The kiss was light, a hummingbird touch, a tentative query. His hand at the back of her head relaxed a little, as if giving her the chance to pull away. But she pressed closer, her lips firmer on his, and he responded instantly. His arm went around her waist, and he pulled her gently against him. His mouth moved over hers, searchingly, learning her shape and softness. Aubrey held herself still, enjoying the sweet caress, until his tongue flicked against her lips. Without thought she parted them, sighing softly and relaxing against him as his tongue slipped inside her mouth.

The kiss could have gone on for hours for all Aubrey was aware. When Robert finally lifted his head, it took her a moment to remember where they were. When she did, she carefully eased back from him, releasing her hold on his shoulders and tossing her head to resettle the hair he had tangled.

Neither spoke; they simply stared at each other, not touching except for his hand, which lingered on her cheek.

"Do you kiss like that all the time," he finally asked, his voice a bit husky, "or was that something special?"

She nodded slowly. "That was something special." She inclined her head toward him, questioning with her eyes.

He smiled, a full, fabulous smile. "It was special for me, too."

Silence fell between them for another minute; then Aubrey shook her head. "We'd better go," she muttered, and he released the Stop button.

Once again, immediately and without sound, the elevator started up. It took only a few more seconds to reach the eleventh floor, then it obediently slid its door open. Aubrey stepped out and began rummaging through her bag for her keys, pretending she couldn't find them so that she wouldn't have to look at Robert. That kiss had definitely been the start of something, but she hoped he wouldn't push it. Her body might say yes, but her mind and heart would know it wasn't right.

When they reached her apartment door, she found her keys and quickly unlocked the two locks. She was about to push the door open, hoping to say good-night from the comparative safety of her well-lit hall, when Robert stopped her. He laid his hand over hers and gently pulled it away from the doorknob.

"Aubrey," he said quietly, in such a wonderful tone that she couldn't help but look up at him. "Don't be nervous. I'm not going to ask for more than you're willing to give. Ever. But before you flee into your apartment, do you suppose you could give me your phone number so I could call you and ask you for a real date?"

Feeling like an absolute fool, Aubrey pulled a pen and some paper from her bag and scribbled down her address, phone number and the number at Alex's. Robert carefully folded the paper and put it in his inside jacket pocket.

"I'll call—" he began, but her fingers on his lips stopped him.

"Don't tell me when you'll call, or even that you will call." She smiled crookedly. "Puts too much pressure on us both."

The furrows in his brow told her he didn't understand what she was saying. But he only kissed her fingers and nodded.

"Good night," she whispered, and stood on her toes and quickly kissed him.

He was even quicker, though, and grabbed her arms and held her in place while he gave her a much more thorough kiss.

"Now *that* was good night," he said as he released her.

She didn't bother to try to get the last word in. She simply slipped inside her apartment and locked the door. It was never a good idea to let a man know just how incoherent his kiss could make you.

3

AUBREY WAS LATE for her date with Robert the following Friday night. He had called her Sunday afternoon and asked to take her out to dinner her first free night. When she had said Friday, he had grunted, paused, then said that would be fine. She'd gotten the feeling he had something else planned for that night, and had been flattered that he would cancel his plans to be with her. However, after she'd hung up, she had decided she had read too much into the whole situation. If Robert had cancelled anything for Friday, it was probably a trip to the dentist.

For the next five and a half days she vacillated between looking forward to seeing Robert and wanting to cancel the date. With the width of the city separating them, she could misremember the intensity of his gaze when he looked at her, convince herself that he wasn't really pursuing her in a wolflike manner, and that his half-joking comments about Sir Galahad didn't have a ring of possessiveness to them. But she couldn't ignore or discount her reaction to him, how any resistance to him melted within seconds of being with him. Always before she had known exactly what was going on in her relationships with men, but with Robert she was thoroughly baffled.

"Nothing would ever work anyhow," she told Maggie almost frantically late Thursday night. "He's East Side lawyer, I'm West Side bartender. We're totally different. He'd never understand—or accept—the way I live."

"So why are you going out with him?" Maggie asked.

"Curiosity? Masochism? Boredom? I don't know. I just don't have any common sense when he's around."

"Sounds better and better all the time. And what's so weird about the way you live?"

THIS IS WHAT'S SO WEIRD, Aubrey thought the next evening as she shooed a few people out of her bedroom. Mitch and Sara Sullivan, the couple who shared the large apartment with her and Maggie, had announced late that afternoon that they were pregnant. Within half an hour, the apartment was filled with an odd assortment of friends and neighbors there to congratulate the happy couple. Aubrey herself had been so caught up in the celebrating that she hadn't noticed the time until there was only half an hour before Robert was due to arrive.

After firmly closing the bedroom doors to both the hall and her living room, she began hurriedly getting ready. Her dress was cranberry colored, had a V-neck, short sleeves and a very simple, straight cut. What made it was a black-leather belt worn low and angled across her hips. She pulled her hair into a chignon and added silver earrings and a matching necklace, bought from a silversmith in New Mexico, and a bit of makeup. Her stockings were black and textured, and she was just slipping into her low-heeled black-leather shoes—

noting with regret that her toenail polish, Wyld Strawberry, clashed with her dress—when the doorbell rang.

"He would be on time," she muttered as she gave herself one last check in the mirror. Satisfied, she opened her bedroom door, only to discover that Mitch had beaten her to the front door.

"Hi, there," he was saying boisterously. "Have some champagne." He shoved a glass at the person hidden behind the open door.

Aubrey rolled her eyes, then quickly stepped across the hall and nudged the grinning Mitch away from the door. "Uh, hello, Robert," she said, trying to gauge his reaction to this peculiar greeting.

He did look a little startled, standing there with a plastic glass of champagne in one hand and a bouquet of flowers in the other. He was still staring at Mitch when Aubrey spoke, but then his eyes shifted to her, and he started to smile. His gaze slowly ran the length of her body, lingering here and there, then just as slowly slid back up.

"I'll drink to *that*," he finally said, toasting her and sipping the champagne.

Mitch turned his flushed face to Aubrey. "He's your date, huh, P.T.?" he said. "Sorry about that. I thought he was one of ours."

"Don't worry about it," she said. "Let me introduce you. Mitch, this is Robert Browning. Robert, this is Mitch Sullivan, one of my roommates. His wife just found out she's pregnant, so we were having a little party."

Robert handed the flowers to Aubrey, then shook Mitch's hand. "Congratulations," he said. "I intended the flowers for you, Aubrey," he added, "but maybe you could share them with the expectant mother."

She smiled. What a nice man, she thought. How did such a good-looking man get to be so nice? "Sure," she said. "Why don't you come in? I'll give you a tour of the apartment, and I'm sure we'll run into Sara somewhere."

Mitch left them to return to his celebrating, and Aubrey started down the hall after closing the door behind Robert. He stopped her, however, catching her wrist and saying, "Just a minute."

She halted instantly, warmth from both his hand and his rich voice washing over her and making her momentarily light-headed. He tugged gently on her arm, turning her and drawing her close to him. For a moment she avoided his eyes, her senses already overwhelmed by his touch, his nearness, the pleasant scent of his after-shave. Then she looked up, and felt light-headed again when she saw the glow in his eyes.

"It may sound crazy," he said, his voice low and deep, "but I've missed you these past few days."

She shook her head and started to answer, but he didn't give her the chance. His head lowered swiftly, his lips catching hers in a firm yet tender kiss. His arms slid around her waist, and she put her arms around his neck, careful to keep the damp end of the paper-wrapped bouquet from his back. The kiss might have gone on for a long time, so wonderful was it, but Aubrey suddenly remembered that she had promised herself this wouldn't happen, that she wouldn't let Robert just take over like this. She pulled away.

His gaze was thoughtful as he looked down at her. Then he nodded as though he now understood something that had been puzzling him. "How about that tour?" he asked.

The apartment was divided in half by one long, wide hallway; the first door on the right was Aubrey's bedroom. It was a large room, done in shades of dusty rose and cream, and opposite the hall door were French doors leading to a terrace. In a corner of the room was a small shelf, out of Merlin's reach, on which sat several glass figurines. Robert paused to admire them, especially a saucy unicorn and a winged fairy, poised for flight. In the center of the wall to the left of the hall door was another door, which led to Aubrey's living room. This was decorated boldly in white, moss green and a vibrant salmon pink and also had a door to the terrace. Robert was surprised to see nearly full tall bookcases against one wall, and even more surprised when he noted that about a third of the books were hardcovers—contemporary best-selling novels, classics and nonfiction books on art and the Victorian era in England. More than half her paperbacks were science fiction and fantasy. He would have loved to browse through the collection, but Aubrey was leading him back into the hall.

There were three doors around the end. The glass one on the right led to Maggie's living-room-bedroom. It was huge, almost as big as Aubrey's two rooms put together, and was done in Oriental black and red. Two doors led off Maggie's room to the terrace. Behind the middle hall door was a small bathroom that connected the two halves of the apartment. Aubrey and Maggie shared this. The door on the left led to a large kitchen that Robert immediately coveted. He wasn't a gourmet cook by any means, but figured if he had a kitchen this size with such an array of pots and pans, a microwave, two toaster ovens and a food processor, he just might be. Aubrey paused in the kitchen to fill two glass vases with the flowers, lovely red and white carnations, that Robert had brought. She left one vase in the kitchen and carried the other with her.

Below the kitchen, more or less opposite the lower half of Maggie's room and the upper half of Aubrey's living room, was Mitch and Sara's living room. At the moment it was filled with people, and all Robert could discern was that the Sullivans liked the color blue, new music and people who wore bright, eccentric clothes and laughed a lot.

As they stood in the doorway, Aubrey gestured to the left, toward the front door. "The next room," she said, "is Mitch and Sara's bedroom, and the last one by the door is their bathroom."

Robert nodded. "Quite a spread. Have you lived here long?"

"I moved in about six years ago, just before rents in this area skyrocketed. That's how I can afford such a luxurious amount of space. I hold the lease, then rent out the rest of the space to roommates. Maggie's been here about two years, and the Sullivans for one."

"Are you that hard to get along with," he asked with a teasing grin, "even in an apartment this size, that no one stays around for long?"

She shrugged, a little uncomfortably, he thought. "I guess I just know people who don't like to stay in one place for very long."

She started into the room, and Robert followed her, wondering if Aubrey and her roommates were a case of opposites attracting or of birds of a feather flocking together.

Aubrey quickly found Sara and introduced Robert to her. He discovered within a few sentences that Sara was a painter and Mitch was a professor of art history at Columbia University. Most of their friends, Sara told him, were artistic types, some good, some bad, some awful, but all great fun. She then introduced him to the two androgynous-looking people beside her. From their names, Robert guessed that one was a woman and one a man, but he wasn't sure which was which. While he was puzzling over this, Maggie joined them, gleefully reintroducing herself to Robert and saying how pleased she was to see him again. Pretending to leer at her voluptuous figure in a tight-fitting black jump suit, he grinned and said, "Likewise."

He chatted with Maggie for a few minutes, then realized that at some point Aubrey had disappeared. He excused himself from Maggie and started working his way around the room, hoping with his superior height to catch a glimpse of her shining dark hair. He found her in a far corner, perched on the arm of a blue chair, chatting with three men—one of whom had his arm around her waist and was trying to ease her body against his.

Robert politely intruded, greeted the three men with a smile that wasn't altogether pleasant, then said to

Aubrey, "Our reservations, dear. We're going to be late."

Suppressing a grin, Aubrey slid off the arm of the chair, then turned to the three men and smiled a bright goodbye to them. Robert followed her through the room, out the door and into her bedroom.

"Phew," she said, leaning down to pet Merlin, who was looking rather kinglike, lying in splendor on a knitted afghan at the foot of Aubrey's bed. "That party's rather like a sixteen-armed octopus."

Robert chuckled, then watched with interest as she pulled her lipstick from a small black purse and began applying it. When he realized he was staring, he quickly turned and looked instead at a painting hanging over a small antique chair in the corner of the room. It was a charming, airy painting of a meadow on a spring day, done in greens and blues and golds. He leaned closer and saw the initials "SS" in one corner.

"Sara's?" he asked, glancing over his shoulder to find Aubrey looking at him.

She nodded. "She gave it to me in lieu of their first month's rent. I think they overpaid me. It's rather good, don't you think?"

"Yes," he said, looking at it again.

"You sound surprised."

"I guess I am, a little." He shrugged and faced Aubrey. "You've got to admit that's a rather odd collection of people in there. And Sara seemed so, well, vague."

Aubrey studied him carefully for a moment. "Not the kind of people you're used to, I'm sure," she said softly; then she smiled. "But if you'd just been told you were pregnant after you'd been trying for a year, you'd probably sound a bit vague, too."

He nodded with mock seriousness. "I'm sure I would."

She laughed and picked up her bag and coat. "Let's go eat," she said.

Again he followed her, and again he wondered, as he glanced back at Mitch and Sara's living room, if birds of a feather did flock together.

THE RESTAURANT Robert had chosen was small and French, with white linen tablecloths and candles and discreet waiters and fabulous food. He found the quiet soothing after the Sullivans' party and was glad to have Aubrey more or less to himself. As she sipped her melon-ball cocktail and studied the menu, he noticed how the candlelight flickered over the pronounced, attractive planes of her face, from her high cheekbones to her almost Roman nose to the beautifully drawn mouth.

"What nationality are you?" he asked suddenly.

She looked up, her face blank for a moment. "Hard to say," she said after a brief pause. "I usually just say Gypsy and leave it at that."

"Gypsy," he repeated musingly. "I can certainly see that. Your dark hair and eyes, your almost olive complexion. Very Mediterranean."

She laughed softly. "You forgot my big nose."

He reached across the table and lightly stroked that nose. "It's just got a lot of character."

"So diplomatic. You *must* be a good lawyer."

He grinned. "I am." Then he became somber and took her hand. "Tell me if I'm trespassing, but why is it hard to say what nationality you are?"

Oh, hell. If anyone else had asked, she would have definitely told him he was trespassing. But not Robert, whose blue eyes gazed at her so sincerely and warmly, whose hand felt strong yet so tender on hers. "I'd never want to see you hurt," he'd said, and she realized with a little shock that she liked that idea, that Robert would protect her from the wayward winds of life that seemed to have blown her hither and yon since the day she was born.

"I was abandoned," she said softly, looking directly at him, "when I was a week old. I was found in a motel room in some small town in Arizona. The woman— girl, actually—who'd rented the room had skipped out that morning. She'd given her name as Aubrey Celia, so when the police took me to the local orphanage, that's the name they gave me."

Her gaze wavered, and she looked away. Robert's hand tightened on hers.

"Needless to say," she went on, staring at the red rose and white baby's breath in the center of their table, "they never located my mother. No one had ever heard of her, the local hospitals had no record of my birth, no one came forward to claim me. Thankfully I was strong and healthy and pretty, the kind of baby people like to adopt. When I was three months old a couple named Jones adopted me. They were in their late twenties and unable to have children. I was the only one they ever adopted."

She looked up again, and was astonished and touched to see sadness and empathy in Robert's eyes. She smiled a little wanly and squeezed his hand. "Don't look like that, Robert," she said. "It happened a long time ago. My foster parents are truly wonderful and I had a . . . good childhood."

He studied her for a moment. There was an odd insistence in her voice, as if she were trying to convince herself as well as him that her childhood had been happy. "It is a sad story, Aubrey," he said finally, "but you're right. It happened years ago. But I'm glad you told me."

"So am I."

They stared at each other for a long time, and Aubrey began feeling light-headed again. She couldn't concentrate on any one thought, and her entire body seemed flushed. Somehow this dinner had changed from a casual event to the beginning of something serious, and she wasn't entirely certain that was wise on her part. Nor was she certain there was anything she could do about it.

By unspoken consent, their conversation during dinner ranged over a variety of impersonal topics, from the merits of a graduate degree to politics and nuclear war and the joys and pitfalls of feminism and sexual freedom. Aubrey was surprised that, for the most part, she and Robert were in agreement. When they did disagree, it wasn't so violently that they couldn't at least discuss the subject. After they were through eating and she was waiting by the curb outside the restaurant while Robert hailed a taxi, she decided dinner had been a very pleasant affair.

And now what, she wondered, watching Robert, admiring his lean, muscular frame, his tailored clothes, the reddish sparkle in his hair under the streetlight. Neither had had coffee or dessert at the restaurant. She really should offer at least the former when they got to her place. Then she remembered the kisses they had shared, felt again the excitement even his light touch sparked within her. *Take it slow, Jones*, she firmly told herself, *and just offer him coffee*.

IT WAS A LITTLE AFTER ELEVEN when they reached her apartment. Robert hadn't hesitated to pick up on her offer of coffee. Yet he didn't kiss her in the elevator, which left her somewhat disappointed. Her apartment was quiet, all the doors shut. There was no light in the Sullivans' area, but they could see through Maggie's glass door that her room was blazing with light.

"Maggie's a night owl," Aubrey said as she led Robert down the hall to the kitchen.

There she quickly made a pot of freshly ground, delicious-smelling coffee—"A mixture of mocha java and Colombian," she said—and fixed a tray with mugs and cream and homemade chocolate-chip cookies and the vase of flowers. When the coffee was ready, she instructed Robert to take the pot and follow her. Since Maggie was probably working, Aubrey decided she and Robert should sit in her bedroom. In the corner of the room, near the French doors, were a tiny round table and two chairs, and she set the tray down there.

As she poured the coffee, Robert studied a small painting he hadn't noticed before. It was in a different style than Sara's, depicting a young woman, dressed in a white Victorian gown, standing by the ocean. But rather than looking out to sea, she had her head tilted to the side, so that she wasn't quite looking over her shoulder. It was as though she knew she would shortly be joined by someone, but was pretending not to watch his approach. The painting had an air of delight and mystery, and Robert imagined the woman was meeting a secret lover.

"Another of Sara's?" he asked, accepting a mug of coffee from Aubrey.

"No," she said, and something in the way her eyes shifted and her mouth twitched made him suspicious. He studied the painting again and could just see, looking like a pattern in the sand, the signature: "A. Jones."

He turned back to her. "Why didn't you tell me you paint?"

She shrugged, gestured for him to sit and sat down herself. "It's what I did when I first came to New York. And I practically starved. My mother's a painter, you see, and I learned from her. Sara's been teaching me a little off and on now, but I really haven't gone back to it for six years."

"But it's important to you," Robert said, listening more to her tone of voice than her words.

"Yes," she admitted, "but so's eating. And I can't just paint as a hobby. It consumes me too much." She hid behind her mug and a cookie, and Robert knew the conversation was over.

For a few minutes they sipped and munched and didn't speak. They both looked out the French doors at the nighttime city spread out below them, the many lights from the streets and the apartments, the occasional glimpse of a person through an uncurtained window.

"The city's fabulous like this," Aubrey said unexpectedly. "It's as though all of it and everyone in it is holding their breath, waiting for something magical to appear, as though secret, wonderful things are just waiting to happen as soon as you turn around. As though Peter Pan is poised outside your window, watching for the chance to slip inside."

Fascinating, Robert thought, noting the gleam in Aubrey's eyes as she revealed her fantasy, watching how her hands fluttered in the air as she spoke, as if they were fairies eager for a chance to explore the night.

"You really love it here, don't you?" he said.

Something flickered in her eyes, like shutters being abruptly closed. He knew instantly that she was regretting her impulsive revelation. "I guess I do," she said slowly. "I've managed to survive for six and a half years here, I have plenty of friends, a job that pays well enough." She shrugged. "What more could you ask for?"

He smiled his half smile. "Do you realize how evasive you are, or is it something that just comes naturally?"

She blinked, then stared at him wide-eyed. No man she had dated had ever called her on her evasiveness. *That's because,* a loud-voiced part of her said, *the men you've dated didn't care about you, only about themselves and their fun. This man cares.* She nodded, remembering his empathy at dinner. Yes, Robert did seem to care.

"Yes, what?" he asked, interpreting her nod as an answer to his question.

"Oh . . . uh, no," she said. "That is, yes, I know how evasive I am, but yes, it also tends to just come naturally."

He drew his brows together in a frown. "*Why* are you so evasive?"

She managed to laugh. "Don't you know better than to ask an evasive person such a direct question? Evasiveness is simply a form of self-defense. Everyone has defense mechanisms. I'm sure even you have a couple."

He shook his head. "Grand master at not answering questions, aren't you?"

"Yes," she said seriously, "and I am evasive, and . . . don't push it, Robert. Don't ask for too much too soon."

He began munching on another cookie. "You're right," he said after a moment. "We have only known each other little more than two weeks." He grinned. "But somehow I've gotten the feeling we've known each other a lot longer than that, that we've already gone through most of the preliminary stages." He stroked her cheek with a lingering hand. "Sorry if I pushed a bit too much."

Bad enough that he was so intuitive about her, then so understanding, but his touch undid her. "Oh, Robert," she whispered, "why are you so nice?"

His hand cupped the back of her neck, and he gently eased her forward as he leaned across the table. Their lips met in a soft, chaste kiss, clung for an instant, and then he said, "You're rather nice yourself."

Her eyes were closed, but she knew he was smiling.

His mouth brushed across hers again, explored one cheek, then returned and settled firmly on her parted lips. His touch was warm, gentle, yet very arousing, and Aubrey suddenly found the table between them a great inconvenience. Robert obviously felt the same way, for they rose together, still kissing, and moved as if by instinct into each other's arms. Aubrey gasped at the wonderful feel of his hard body against hers, at his hand running up and down her back, at his other hand nestling in the curve of her waist. Her own hands were tangling in his silky, thick hair.

"Aubrey," he moaned. His mouth left hers and began exploring, from her jaw to her throat and downward, as his hand at her waist slid upward. With deliberate slowness it traveled up her ribs, seeming to stop to count each one until Aubrey felt she would scream from frustration. Finally he cupped one needy breast in his hand, his thumb stroking the hardening nipple.

"You feel so good," he whispered, nuzzling her throat.

She leaned her head back and said, "Mmm."

He pressed his body more firmly against hers, letting her know how much he wanted her and bending her backward over his arm. She clung to his shoulders, unconcerned that he might drop her. She was too busy enjoying his caresses, his warm tongue investigating the V-neck of her dress, his hand learning quite thoroughly the shape and feel of her breast. Besides, she knew he had turned so that the bed was directly below her.

His mouth began traveling upward again, and his hand left her breast and started sliding downward. As his mouth reached her ear, his hand found the belt at the side of her lean hip.

"This belt of yours," he murmured as his tongue traced her ear, "has driven me crazy all night."

"Oh?" she managed to gasp as he shifted his body against hers, moving to the side, pressing his arousal against her thigh and giving his hand access to the front of her body.

"Yes, oh," he said, and his hand followed the leather across her belly to the buckle. It rested there for a moment, and he said, "It entices a man in the most indecent way, this belt of yours, with its buckle lying right here—" he pressed his palm against the buckle "—and making a man wonder about what's just below it."

His fingers spread downward, across her lower body, curving under to graze the already hot, moist place between her thighs. She gasped at the explosion within her, as though the small fire Robert had lit with his first sweet kiss had finally reached a cache of TNT. Tremors shook her body as passion flowed throughout, and she clung even more fiercely to him. With a muttered exclamation he tightened his hold, both arms going around her and drawing her upright against him so that their bodies nestled together, his hardness finding a welcome against her softness. He kissed her, his mouth feverish on hers, his tongue exploring with rapid thoroughness. She responded wholeheartedly, her hands roaming up and down his back as she made small sounds of satisfaction and desire in the back of her throat.

"My Lord, woman," he finally muttered, his breathing harsh. "I want you very, very much." His hands cupped her hips, pressed her more firmly against him, brushed her back and forth across his pelvis.

"Robert . . ." She took a deep, hopefully steadying breath. "I do, too, but not . . . not yet."

Resting her hands lightly on his shoulders, she stared into his eyes, which revealed the strength of his need and passion. Slowly, though, as he returned her stare, the passion ebbed, and she could feel his body relax— a little.

He let out his breath in a long, slow sigh. "You're right," he said, then grinned. "Damn it," he added mildly.

She smiled. "I know."

His hand dropped from her hips, and he stepped back. "I should go before I want to do this all over again." He walked back to the table, polished off another cookie and finished his coffee in two gulps. "My mother always told me to clean my plate," he explained to an amused Aubrey.

"There are three cookies left. Want to take them for that long cab ride home?"

He looked at the cookies for a moment, then said, "Naw. Save them for when I come back."

No way was she going to ask when that would be. She turned and led him to the front door. "I had a lovely time," she said. "Thank you."

"Thank *you*," he said. "I had a great time, too, party and all."

She glanced behind him to the Sullivans' now-quiet living room. "Oh, right, the party," she said weakly.

He looked at her curiously, then asked, "When can I see you again?"

She closed her eyes and ran her schedule for the following week through her head. "I'm free Tuesday," she said, opening her eyes.

"May I see you Tuesday night?" he asked formally.

"Most certainly," she replied. "How about a movie?"

"Great." He eyed her slyly. "And take-out Chinese?"

"Oh, no. Is that one of your weaknesses, too?" He grinned and nodded. "Well, at least we have one thing in common."

He smiled lazily and easily pulled her into his arms. "Oh, I can think of one or two other things we have in common," he said, his voice low and intimate.

His kiss was brief but devastating. When he released her mouth, Aubrey was embarrassed to find she was clinging weakly to him.

"Yes, well," she said, stepping out of his embrace and smoothing down her dress, "perhaps we do have one other thing in common."

He chuckled and lifted her chin up to drop a quick kiss on her lips. "I'll see you Tuesday. Good night...and pleasant dreams."

"Good night," she murmured.

She watched him until the elevator arrived and, with a wave, he stepped into it and disappeared. Then she heavily closed the door, flinching a little at the loud clunks the locks made when she refastened them. She carried the remains of their coffee and cookies back to the kitchen, and while she was rinsing the mugs Maggie appeared by her side.

"Have a nice evening?" she asked cheerfully.

Aubrey looked up. "Oh, Maggie," she said, "you know how I covet that robe. Why do you insist on wearing it around me? To torture me?"

Maggie glanced down at her red Oriental silk robe with embroidered dragons in gold crawling all over it, then back at Aubrey. "Quit evading the issue. Did you have a nice evening?"

Aubrey couldn't hide her smile at Maggie's steamroller tactics. "Yes, I had a nice evening," she replied dutifully.

"Did he make a pass at you?"

"Really, Maggie!"

"Is that a yes or a no?"

Aubrey laughed. "You just don't stop, do you? Here, have a cookie. And yes, he did."

Maggie nodded sagely as she chomped on the cookie. "As I suspected. That's why he left so soon."

Aubrey felt a flash of anger that Maggie had noticed when they'd come home and when Robert had left. Of course, even in an apartment this size it was impossible to keep people's comings and goings a secret, and Aubrey had never really minded before that her roommates knew how long a date lasted. Why now did she feel her privacy had been violated?

Some of what she was feeling must have shown in her face, for Maggie took a few hasty steps backward. "I think I'll go on to bed now," she said. "Glad you had a good time, P.T. I like Robert. G'night."

"'Night," Aubrey said. Rather absently she put the last two cookies away, then took one back out and ate it. She brushed a few crumbs off the table so as not to encourage the roaches, then returned to her bedroom.

Merlin was already asleep on the afghan and scarcely stirred when Aubrey sat down on the edge of the bed, directly in front of her full-length mirror. Without thinking, she took the pins out of her hair, then combed it through with her fingers until it lay heavily on her shoulders. She continued staring at herself for a moment, then abruptly stood up. Her gaze focused on the belt buckle and the tab end of the belt, which cut diagonally across her body. Had Robert really found her so enticing, had her outfit really driven him crazy all evening? She closed her eyes as she remembered the feel of his lips on hers, his hands discovering her body, his palm pressing against that buckle while his fingers . . .

She shook her head and opened her eyes. She would not dwell on thoughts of Robert. She was a firm believer in the adage: be careful what you dream; you may get it. She didn't want to dream about Robert, about what it would be like to have his mouth and hands explore more of her, to fix him coffee in the morning as well as at night, to have him pick her up at work every night.

"No," she said aloud, shaking her head again. Although Robert wasn't a stereotypical, stuffy East Side lawyer, she still didn't think he was her type. Her type would have been comfortable at the Sullivans' party, fit right in, been one of the crowd. But then, did she want someone who was just one of the crowd? Oh, that was ridiculous. The bottom line was that despite the intangible but nonetheless obvious bond that had been forged between her and Robert when she'd told him about her natural mother, she was just plain lousy at anything long term, at commitment, at hanging in there for the long haul. Why else her myriad boyfriends? Why else nine jobs in six years? Her job at Alex's was going for the record—she'd been there for eight months already.

She sighed and quickly stripped off her clothes. Dressed in a pair of silky pajamas, she opened one of the French doors, caressed the soft yet crisp petals of the carnations, turned out the light and slid into bed. Merlin immediately settled himself against her body, and she idly stroked the cat's furry head.

"Whaddaya think, Merlin?" she whispered. "A man like that could cause me trouble—that's a line from a song, isn't it—but I'll still see him again. I never thought I'd want a knight in shining armor, but it would be nice to have someone to lean on for a little while. However, it seems to me knights are notorious for moving on to bigger and better challenges and conquests all the time. Maybe Robert and I are more alike than I think."

Merlin just purred, as usual, in response. Frustrated at her inability to see into the future, Aubrey rolled onto her side, clutching her pillow and sighing when Merlin resettled against her stomach and drawn-up legs. She would, she thought as her eyes drifted closed, have preferred Robert.

4

ROBERT ARRIVED at Aubrey's at 6:30 on the dot Tuesday night. She was pleased with her casual greeting of him. When she had awakened Saturday morning she'd been disconcerted by the memory of dreams about a knight with pure blue eyes who sometimes rode a unicorn, sometimes consorted with Merlin, sometimes kissed a black-haired maid. By Monday evening, however, she'd convinced herself that she could handle Robert. So what if he was different from other men she'd gone out with? She still doubted he would be interested in her for very long. He might have fun playing Sir Galahad, but once he realized how very capable she was of taking care of herself, and how settled she was in her own life, he would move on to easier conquests.

They perused the menu from a nearby Chinese restaurant that delivered and discovered they had very similar tastes. They ate their dinner sitting on the floor in her living room, the food set up on the coffee table.

"I have guests for dinner so rarely," Aubrey explained, "I've never bothered to get a decent dining table."

While they ate, they discussed trivial matters like favorite restaurants and favorite movies. They heard the front door open and close several times, and Robert remarked on it.

"Do you ever see your roommates?" he asked, looking toward the closed living-room door.

"Well, we're bound to run into each other every now and again." She took a bite of a fried dumpling and smiled beatifically. "It works out very well. Everyone pretty much keeps to his or her own space, and we're more like friendly neighbors than roommates."

And you do like your own space, don't you, Aubrey? Robert thought. He was tempted to speak the thought, but instead just nodded and turned back to his chicken Hunan.

By eight they had finished their dinner, stacked the dishes in the sink and were ready to go to a movie.

"Let me just feed Merlin," Aubrey said, pulling a can of cat food from a cupboard.

"Where has he been?" Robert asked. "I haven't seen him all evening."

She shrugged as she fit the can onto the electric opener. "He gets into nonpeople moods sometimes," she said over the whirring of the opener. She began scooping the food into the cat's dish, then looked around in surprise. "He should have shown up by now, though. It's way past his usual eating time, and he comes running when he hears the can opener."

She set the dish down on the floor and called for Merlin in a high-pitched voice. No response. She whistled and called again. When Merlin still didn't appear, she began to grow concerned.

Leaving the kitchen, she tapped on the glass door to Maggie's room. "Maggie, is Merlin in there with you?"

Maggie took a quick look around the room, then shook her head. "No. Did you lose him?"

"I hope not."

She walked down the hall to her own rooms, but a thorough search there didn't turn up the cat. She met Maggie in the hall.

"He's not in Mitch and Sara's rooms," Maggie said.

"He hasn't shown up here," Robert added from the kitchen door.

"Oh, no. You don't suppose he got out when someone opened the front door, do you?" Aubrey said.

"It's happened before," Maggie said. A ringing noise sounded faintly from her room. "Whoops. There's my phone. Let me just answer that, and then I'll help you look."

Aubrey looked at Robert. "Want to come?" she asked.

"Sure." He strode down the hall to her. "How far could he have gone?" he asked as she opened the door.

"You'd be surprised." She propped the door open in case Merlin came back, and they set off.

Five minutes later they'd made a circuit of the entire eleventh floor, which was much larger than Robert had thought, without success.

"Now what?" Robert asked.

Aubrey shrugged. "We try again. When we're fairly certain he's not on this floor, we'll check the stairwell."

"But the stairs have a door. Isn't it kept closed?"

"Sometimes people use the stairs if they're just going up or down a flight or two to visit someone. He could have slipped through then."

"How many times has Merlin done this?"

"Countless," she said dryly.

Their second time around the floor, they met one of Aubrey's neighbors.

"Have you lost your cat again?" the elderly man asked, poking his head out his open door.

"I'm afraid so, Mr. Windsor," Aubrey said. "You haven't seen or heard him, have you?"

"Nope. But I'll help you look, if you like."

"Oh, would you? I'd really appreciate it."

"Sure thing. Ellen," he called back into the apartment, "come on out here. Aubrey's cat's missin' again."

Mr. Windsor stepped out of his apartment, and Robert tried not to stare at the man's exquisite velvet smoking jacket—or at his much-worn plain cotton trousers. The woman named Ellen followed Mr. Windsor, and she, Robert noted, was also oddly dressed in a silk caftan with cheap foam-rubber slippers on her feet and brightly colored rag curlers in her hair.

"I'm so sorry Merlin's missing, dear," the older woman said to Aubrey. "Where would you like us to look?"

"Thanks so much for your help, Mrs. Bellingford," Aubrey said. "If you wouldn't mind asking the other neighbors if they've seen Merlin, Robert and I will check out the stairs."

"Robert?" Mrs. Bellingford turned to him, blinked her bright blue eyes once, then said to Aubrey, "That sounds fine, dear. Come along, Alfred."

As the couple walked away, Robert turned to Aubrey. "Why is one Windsor and one Bellingford?" he whispered.

"They're living in sin," she whispered back. "He's a widower, but she's still married. Her husband won't give her a divorce."

"How long have they been living together?"

"They were here when I first moved in, six years ago. Come on," she said in a normal voice. "Let's go check the stairs."

They separated at the stairs, Robert going down and Aubrey going up. When he'd reached the ninth floor, Robert heard a man above him shout, "Merlin? Is that you down there?"

"No," Robert called back. "I'm looking for him, too."

"Oh." There was a pause. "Where's Aubrey?"

"I'm up here." Her voice floated down to them.

"Well, if one of you is up and one of you is down, what should I do?"

"Just hold the door open and call to him, would you, Bruce?" Aubrey suggested.

Who was Bruce, Robert wondered, then continued on his way down as the unseen man started calling the cat's name. When Robert reached the eighth floor, the stairwell door opened.

"You Robert?" a man with a punk haircut and one dangling earring asked.

Robert nodded, too bemused to speak.

"I'm Ted, Bruce's roommate." He held out his hand and Robert automatically shook it. "Aubrey said I should go down the next few floors, and you should go back up. We do this about once a month, so we've got a real good system."

Robert nodded again and started back up. Once a month, he repeated silently. Good Lord.

At the eleventh floor, he saw the man he presumed was Bruce, holding the door open and still calling the cat. Robert had been expecting a clone of Ted and was amazed to see that Bruce had short, Yuppie-style hair, was wearing a plain cotton shirt, jeans and Topsiders.

"Bruce?" he asked.

"Yeah. You must be Robert. I don't know where Aubrey is, but we've got the stairs covered now, so you can hang out here on the eleventh floor."

"Fine," Robert said, and stepped into the hallway.

Good Lord, he thought again. What was going on? He saw at least four people walking down the hall in one direction, another three going another way. One person was dribbling some sort of green herb onto the floor as she went.

"What's that?" Robert asked, nodding toward the woman.

"Catnip," Bruce said. "Merlin loves the stuff."

Robert nodded. "Of course."

He walked down the hall to Aubrey's apartment, where he found Maggie standing in the open doorway by a bowl of cat food.

"Hi," she said. "I see you were relieved of stair duty."

"Don't you think all these people—" he gestured vaguely "—just scare Merlin and make him that much less likely to show up?"

"I doubt it. He probably loves the excitement. He'll show when he gets hungry enough. And everyone has a little fun this way. We probably have the friendliest floor in the entire building."

"I'll bet," he muttered. "Aubrey certainly does collect them."

Maggie looked shrewdly at Robert. "Does that bother you?"

He shrugged. "Not really. I just wish she'd let me in." He smiled wryly. "Would you believe I was really looking forward to being alone with her in a dark movie theater, just like a high-school kid trying to get away from his parents?"

Maggie laughed. "I believe it." Then she added seriously, "Give her time, Robert. She's never known anyone like you before."

He was about to answer when someone yelled, "I found him!"

"Where?" several other people called—then everyone was hurrying toward Mrs. Bellingford. She was walking down the hall to Aubrey's apartment, proudly holding the cat in her arms. Merlin, Robert noted, was looking rather pleased with himself.

Aubrey appeared from another hallway and held out her arms for her cat. "Oh, you naughty thing, Merlin," she said as Mrs. Bellingford passed him to her. "Were you so bored that you had to cause a little excitement for everyone?" She cuddled the cat, who started purring very loudly, then turned to the people gathered in the hall. "Thank you all very, very much. You were splendid, responding to the call to arms so quickly."

"Our pleasure, dear Aubrey," Mr. Windsor said. "What else are neighbors for?"

They all began to disperse, most everyone coming up to Aubrey to pet and scold Merlin. Finally Aubrey and Robert were alone inside the apartment. Even Maggie had disappeared.

"Well," Aubrey said, not quite looking at Robert, "that's one way to spend an evening. I guess we missed the movie. Sorry about all that."

"Are you?" he asked softly.

She set Merlin down and looked at Robert questioningly. "What do you mean?"

"Whether consciously or not, you very handily avoided being alone with me."

She set her hands on her hips and tilted her head back, looking at him cockily. "Are you implying that I'm afraid to be alone with you?" Her voice was mocking, but inside she was thinking, *He's right, he's absolutely right.*

"Afraid isn't exactly the word I'd use," he said, taking a step closer to her. She refused to step back, but some of her cockiness wilted. "Or maybe you're not so much afraid of me as you are of yourself, of what would happen inside if you for once freed yourself." He came even closer.

"F-freed myself?" she sputtered, still refusing to retreat. She grabbed hold of some of her fading cockiness and said, "I'm one of the freest spirits I know."

He shook his head. "I'm not talking about free spirits. I'm talking about releasing what's hidden deep inside you, sharing it with another person, not retreating into this madcap world where everyone just accepts you at face value and no one tries to probe beneath the surface."

She could think of half a dozen retorts, defenses, but couldn't vocalize one of them. Robert had come as close as he could, and his body was lightly touching hers. She was aware of the warmth of that body, of the even rhythm of his breathing. Mostly, though, she was aware of the challenging look in his eyes. She met his look directly, almost defiantly. She saw his challenge fade, melt into something else that she couldn't name, didn't have time to figure out, for his eyes closed and his head lowered. His mouth was on hers, and she didn't want to think anymore. He gathered her close to him. Both his embrace and kiss were tender. His arms simply enfolded her, his hands not traveling over her to incite a passionate fire in her. His lips brushed across hers, kissing from one corner of her mouth to the other. His tongue gently wet her lips but didn't slip between them. After one last sweet kiss, he released her.

"That's not so scary, is it?" he asked, a trace of humor in his deep voice.

She shook her head, unable to speak. How could such a placid, almost innocent embrace arouse her so? His thumb smoothed one of her cheeks, and she rubbed against his hand.

"Don't look at me like that, Aubrey," he said, sounding strained. "I'm tempted to sweep you off your feet and carry you to your bed, but it's too soon."

At the mention of her bed, she snapped out of the sensual haze Robert had captured her in. "How gentlemanly of you," she murmured. "Or should I say knightly?"

He inclined his head. "A knight is always bound to protect his lady, even from himself."

She laughed at his formal tone, even as a thrill passed through her at the thought of being Robert's lady.

He glanced at his watch. "I should prob—"

He was interrupted by the sound of a key being inserted in the lock on the other side of the apartment door.

"It's open!" Aubrey called. "Probably Mitch and Sara," she added to Robert.

"I'm glad they didn't arrive a few minutes earlier," he said, winking.

She grinned, then turned to greet her roommates.

Robert left a few minutes later, feeling again rather like a high-school student. Aubrey's friends, though, were more a deterrent to romance than any of his adolescent girlfriends' parents had been. Or maybe Aubrey herself was the deterrent.

During the cab ride home, and while he was getting ready for bed, Robert pondered the problem. Aubrey felt they were too different and had been letting him know that in various subtle ways. The Sullivans' party and Merlin's being lost had coincidentally happened during their two dates, but he figured that if those situations hadn't been ready-made, Aubrey would have found some way to dissuade him with examples of her unorthodox life.

What she didn't realize, and this thought made him smile, was that he was attracted to that unpredictability in her. His own life left little room for such carefree, even comical, happenings. He admitted he had been startled, somewhat disconcerted, by the way Aubrey lived, but he knew now he wouldn't have her any other way. If only he could get past her barricades, her evasiveness, and convince her to trust him, to open up to him. In a way, he thought as he climbed into bed, she was still a damsel in distress, locked away in some tower. That appealed to his newly awakened sense of chivalry, and he smiled. He'd have to brush up on Camelot, Merlin and Arthur and Guinevere. Especially Guinevere.

NOT SURPRISINGLY, when the alarm woke him the next morning, Robert's first thought was of Aubrey. While he showered, shaved, dressed and gulped a cup of coffee, he had to restrain himself from calling her. She might still be asleep, since she didn't have to go to work in the morning. And therein, he thought as he slipped on his suit coat and picked up his briefcase, lay the rub. He worked all day; she worked all night. Seeing her only two nights a week and maybe part of Saturday and Sunday simply wouldn't be enough. He'd never storm the tower that way.

As he strode toward Second Avenue to catch a southbound cab, he considered the merits of taking this relationship slow and easy. Then he thought of the men at the bar and at the Sullivans' party who had flirted with her, thought of her hesitancy with him, and knew that nothing short of an all-out siege would suit his purposes. With an imperious wave he flagged down a cab, then began plotting his campaign during the death-defying ride downtown.

AUBREY TENDED BAR on Wednesday evenings. She rather liked the off nights like this one, when there were enough customers to keep her occupied, yet not so many that she couldn't enjoy herself. Tonight both the dining room and the bar were about half full, which was just right for Aubrey. She divided her time between mixing drinks, chatting with the maître d' and the patrons at the bar, and thinking about Robert. She wasn't sure if she'd truly expected him to call that day, but she was sure, disconcertingly so, that she was disappointed that he hadn't. She told herself that was ridiculous, that a couple of dates didn't lead to daily phone calls, but that didn't make her feel any better.

The after-work crowd at the bar cleared out by eight o'clock, leaving only a few people for Aubrey to serve. There were no late diners, so except for an occasional liqueur or Irish coffee, there were no drink orders for the dining room. By eight-fifteen Aubrey was perched on a little stool at the far end of the bar, one eye on her customers, the other on the book she was reading. When she heard the door open five minutes later, she looked up with a smile. The smile faltered a little when she saw that the customer was Robert. Good heavens, she thought as she stuffed the book under the bar and stood up, she'd hoped for a phone call, not an out-and-out in-person appearance. As he settled himself on the stool directly opposite her, she made a little show of wiping down the bar, wondering as she did why her hands were shaking slightly.

"Hi, Robert," she said after a moment's pause.

"Hi, Aubrey." That voice, hot-fudge sauce over vanilla ice cream.

"What can I get you?"

"An Irish coffee, with Jameson's and Kahlua. Hold the whipped cream."

She nodded and quickly fixed the drink. Amazing, she thought. He even liked his Irish coffee the same way she did. She set the mug down in front of him and stayed there while he tasted it.

"Just right," he said.

She smiled, wondering why in the world she was so pleased with such a simple compliment. "What brings you all the way over to the West Side, Robert?" she asked.

He grinned. "What do you think?"

A vision flashed through her mind of her in his arms, bent backward over her bed, his hands . . . his lips . . . She tossed her head and said, "Alex's coffee."

Robert chuckled. "Not even close." He grew more serious. "How've you been, Aubrey?"

She idly began rearranging the swizzle sticks and fruit slices. "You make it sound as if we've been apart for months, not just a day."

"What a great opening for a corny line like, 'It seems like it's been months.' But I won't say it; I'm not that tacky." He paused. "I will say I can't understand why you're so nervous, why you won't look at me. Aubrey—" he took hold of one of her hands "—are you upset, sorry about something that happened last night, or even last Friday night?"

She shook her head. She couldn't tell him that when he'd sat down, she'd had a sudden, fierce longing for this to happen every night, for Robert to be an inextricable part of her life. *But he can't be,* she told herself. *It simply wouldn't work.* She forced a smile. "It's just a little slow in here tonight, and I'm kind of bored. I guess that makes me edgy."

He nodded, but she didn't think he believed her. 'As your official knight in shining armor," he said, "I should be able to do something to help you, but I'm afraid I'd just as soon the bar was completely empty so I could have you all to myself."

"Not very noble of you, Sir Lancelot," she said, thankful her tone was light and teasing.

"Sir Lancelot? Is that how you see me?"

"As opposed to Sir Galahad?" She couldn't keep a laugh from sputtering out. "The virgin knight? Not hardly."

Hmm, Robert thought. He really did need to brush up on his Camelot. He'd forgotten that interesting little point about Galahad. "Did Lancelot ever go after the Holy Grail?"

Aubrey frowned as she thought. "I think so. I think most of them did. But Galahad was the one who succeeded." She looked questioningly at Robert. "What's the Holy Grail got to do with anything?"

He opened his mouth to answer, but she noticed a customer signaling her. "Just a moment," she said to Robert, and walked down the bar.

As Aubrey waited on the other man, Robert sipped his coffee and thought about Sir Lancelot. He wasn't sure that was the persona he wanted to take on. After all, that knight had been an adulterer, and with the queen, no less. He was trying to remember any of the other knights of the Round Table when Aubrey returned.

"Of course," she said, as if they hadn't been interrupted, "according to T. H. White, Lancelot was ugly, rather like an ape."

Robert frowned. "But in the movie—"

She dismissed the movie with the wave of a hand. "Hollywood," she said, sniffing. "In real life you'd be hard-pressed to find a man of Lancelot's talents who also looked like Tom Selleck." *Oh, yeah?* a voice in her head said. *What about the man in front of you?*

"Real life?" that man repeated, sounding amused. "And do you call Camelot real life, too?"

"Why not?" she said, only half-teasingly. "What's wrong with twenty years of peace, or however long Arthur managed to hang it all together?"

"Nothing's wrong with it, but Merlin? He's real life?"

She shrugged, focusing her gaze on something above his head, not looking at him. "Why not? I mean, not that I believe in magic, but—" She stopped, puzzled by herself. What was she saying—and why was she saying it to Robert?

He grabbed one of her hands again, squeezing it lightly. "I think maybe you do believe, Aubrey. I think somewhere deep inside you, Merlin and Tinker Bell are alive and well."

She pulled her hand away, irritated with both of them. What a ridiculous idea, believing in Tinker Bell. Another customer signaled her, wanting a refill, and Aubrey walked away from Robert without replying.

Robert didn't feel slighted. Rather he was smiling at himself in the mirror behind the bar, very pleased. He felt he had just learned something significant about Aubrey, although he wasn't sure how it fit in with everything else he'd discovered about her. Of course, he knew she didn't truly believe in Merlin and Tinker Bell. What person who had lived in New York for more than six years could? Still, she did have a cat named

Merlin and glass figurines of fairies and unicorns. He guessed that there might be some small part of her, perhaps a part that had never grown up, that was still looking for magic, hoping against hope that it would appear. She'd called herself a Gypsy over dinner that night, and even that was old-world romantic, considering the Gypsies' reputation for fortune-telling.

Seeing that she was going to continue to ignore him for a little while, he decided to put into action the next step in his siege. He picked up his coffee and strolled into the dining room in search of Alex.

Aubrey suspiciously watched him leave. Was he having dinner there, she wondered. Meeting someone, perhaps? *Don't be silly,* she scolded herself. To use his own words, Robert wouldn't be so tacky. He would, however, she thought as she polished glasses and pushed them into the rack above her head, keep digging at this whole magic business. He seemed to think she really did believe in it, that she expected Merlin— and she didn't mean her cat—to saunter into the bar any day now. How absurd. All right, maybe that was what had attracted her to all those ex-boyfriends over the years, their romantic, idealistic belief in something mystical beyond themselves that could make life better. Still, *she* didn't believe that. Her feet were planted firmly on the ground.

But she was uneasy as she walked back to her stool and picked up her book, as though some potentially dangerous part of her, hiding deep inside until now, was demanding recognition.

5

THURSDAY NIGHT was much busier than Wednesday, and Aubrey didn't have too much time to dwell on matters outside of Alex's. Still, that didn't keep her thoughts from turning often to Robert. Although he'd come back to the bar the previous evening after talking to Alex, it had been for only a few minutes. His goodbye had been casual, as though they were nothing more than acquaintances, and he'd said nothing else about the mythical Merlin—nor about when he'd see her again. He hadn't called that day and by one o'clock he hadn't dropped in to the bar, either.

He probably thinks you're certifiable, Aubrey thought as she wiped down the bar. There were only two customers left in the entire place, a man and a woman sitting at one end of the bar. They seemed to be very involved with each other, and had been for three hours.

As she was drying her hands on a clean cloth, Aubrey saw Alex walk into the bar and approach her.

"Busy night, Aubrey," he said.

She nodded wearily. "And just about over, thank heavens."

He glanced down the bar to the couple. "They should just stop this negotiating, pick a place—his or hers—and go there."

Aubrey leaned against the bar, resting her chin on a propped-up hand. "Oh, I don't know, Alex. It must be a little rough starting an affair, if that's what they're doing, on a weeknight. The morning after is tough enough as it is without two people having to rush around getting ready for work."

"Ah. And do you have so much experience with these mornings after, Aubrey?"

"Really, Alex," she chided him. "What do you think I am?"

"I think," he said grandly, "that you are a woman in need of a vacation."

"What?"

"So I am sending you on a vacation. Now. Tonight."

"What? What are you talking about? No one's sending me anywhere.

Alex didn't answer. He just nodded toward the door behind her. Aubrey turned and saw Robert. He was wearing the same jeans and London Fog jacket he'd had on when they'd first met, but a plain cotton shirt had replaced the sweater. His hair was mussed, as though he'd just come in from sailing, his smile wide, and his eyes were sparkling. Dangling from his right hand was a set of keys that Aubrey recognized as the extra ones to her car; she had given them to Maggie.

"Ready to go, Aubrey?" he asked.

"Ready to— What the—" She turned to her boss. "Alex, what is going on here?"

Alex just grinned and shrugged.

"It's nothing illegal, Aubrey," Robert said. She turned again to see that he had crossed the room to the bar. "This knight in shining armor is simply taking advantage of the clause in the code of chivalry that says he can ride off into the sunset with the damsel he's just rescued from distress."

"I think you're mixing your folklore there," she said dryly.

He shrugged. "Ride off into the dawn, then, which is actually more accurate. Now—"

"But I can't just up and go on vacation," she burst out. "I mean, Alex, don't I have to give you fair warning? And—and what are you doing with my car, Robert Browning? And I would need to pack. What about Merlin? And where are we going?"

Robert chuckled. "Calm down, Aubrey. I've already informed Alex that you're taking a week's vacation, and he's sending you off with his blessings. Maggie got your car for me, and she also packed for you. Merlin's waiting in the car right now. And as far as where we're going, it's a surprise. All I'll tell you is that we're headed north."

AUBREY DIDN'T SPEAK during the entire trip out of New York State, except to mutter occasionally to Merlin. She'd taken him out of his carrier as soon as she'd gotten in the car, and he had happily settled on her lap. He made a few attempts to check out Robert's lap, but Aubrey firmly held him back.

She wasn't refraining from talking because she didn't know what to say, or because she wanted to give Robert the silent treatment. She had plenty to say and wasn't averse to saying it—if she could just figure out what to say *first*, and whether or not she wanted to hear what Robert had to say. Thinking it all through, there seemed to be only one explanation for this elaborate kidnapping. Robert was determined to establish a serious relationship between them.

She reconsidered. No, he could just be interested in a hot and heavy, but brief, affair. But then Robert didn't seem like the type for a hot and heavy affair. Her first supposition, that he was interested in starting something serious between them, seemed most accurate, and that didn't sit well with her. As the car whizzed up the New England Thruway toward Connecticut, she felt a definite tightening of her stomach from emotion. But which one? Happiness or fear? Anticipation or anxiety?

She risked a glance at Robert. She had been right—his nose was perfect in profile. Of course, the rest of him wasn't so bad, either. For a minute she forgot about her clenched stomach and her irritation at Robert's high-handed actions and simply admired the man. He really was quite attractive, and more than that, his character seemed to show through—his strength and humor and sensitivity. And virility and sensuality. Aubrey felt heat rising in her as she remembered the passionate interlude in her bedroom a week earlier, how easily and quickly she'd lost control of herself in this man's arms. It was definitely, she decided as her gaze lingered on his beautiful mouth, anxiety that was tightening her stomach.

At that moment Robert turned to her. Whichever of her confused feelings was showing on her face, it brought a smile to his lips.

"How ya' doin'?" he asked softly.

"Robert," she said, her voice a little shaky, "where are we going?" Even as she asked the question, she realized it could be taken two ways.

Apparently he picked up on that, for his answer could be taken two ways, as well. "Someplace nice," he said, his gaze warm and comforting. "You'll like it."

She digested that in silence, noting absentmindedly when they entered Connecticut, stopped to pay tolls, passed one of the few other cars on the road. Finally, as they approached New Haven, she came to terms with this rather bizarre situation. She had to admit she was intrigued—where could they be going? And just because she and Robert were going somewhere together, alone, didn't mean that anything serious was absolutely, positively going to happen between them. They could end up hating each other in a day or two. It was just a vacation, she told herself, and Robert was certainly too much of a gentleman to force himself on her, either physically or otherwise. He might be driving the car, but that didn't mean he was fully in control. Certain that she could handle Robert and herself, she finally relaxed in her seat and allowed herself a small smile of anticipation.

"How far are we going?" she asked.

He smiled his half smile. "Wouldn't you like to know?"

"I'm not trying to find out where we're going," she said, pretending to be affronted. "I just want to know what the chances are of your falling asleep at the wheel and driving us off the road."

"Slim," he said. "I had a long nap this evening while you were slaving away in your bar."

"Well, all right. But if you do start to feel sleepy. . ."

"I'll pull over."

"I could drive."

He laughed. "No way. Not that I think you'd turn the car around and head back to New York, you understand."

"Of course I wouldn't," she exclaimed, not having to pretend offense this time. "I haven't had a real vacation in a long time."

He gave her a speculative glance. "Sorry. I wasn't sure if you were still upset. And I'm sorry if I did seem a little arrogant, just sweeping you off like that, but I assure you my intentions were—are—honorable."

"Honorable, huh? How dull and disappointing."

"Yes, you are feeling better," he said, chuckling. "Tell me about your night at work."

Aubrey described the typical after-work crowd that had been at Alex's that night—"Most of the people in New York seem to think the weekend starts on Thursday night," she said as an aside—and then mentioned the couple who had sat in the corner most of the evening. She repeated her conversation with Alex, and only when she got to the part about how tough the morning after can be did she realize she was in trouble.

"You speak of these mornings after with a great deal of authority," Robert said, trying to sound like a pompous father.

"I'm sure you've had more of them than I have," she said tartly.

He raised a brow and glanced at her. "So defensive," he murmured. "I wonder why."

"It's just that," she said, trying to force some lightness into her voice, "I make it a practice not to discuss old boyfriends with new boyfriends."

"Am I your boyfriend?" he asked.

It should have sounded silly and high-schoolish, a man in his thirties asking if he was her boyfriend, but it didn't. It sounded sweet—and tantalizing.

"Maybe, Robert," she said softly. "Maybe."

Their conversation lagged after that. They talked about the emptiness of the road at this early-morning hour, the delightfully warm weather, Himalayan cats in general and Merlin in particular. Robert noticed the long gaps between their comments and finally, as they neared the Massachusetts border, suggested to Aubrey that she try to sleep. She protested that she should stay awake to make sure *he* stayed awake, but she was already half asleep, anyway, and when he just looked at her, she reclined her seat, crumpled up his windbreaker to use as a pillow, and fell into a light sleep in less than two minutes.

Robert smiled as he heard her breathing slow and deepen. He had to admit she'd taken the kidnapping better than he'd thought she would. He wished he knew what she'd been thinking during that seemingly interminable drive out of New York. Obviously she'd decided to accept this awkward situation with grace, but why, he wondered, did she suppose he'd done it? Because he was just impetuous, given to crazy, reckless behavior? No, she must know him better than that. Because he wanted to have a wild, passionate, week-long affair with her? No, she had probably figured out that if that was what he wanted, he wouldn't have stopped—at least not so quickly—last Friday night.

He looked at her, at her dark head turned away from him, her face nestled in his jacket. There was something so natural and endearing about that, and he felt something in him—his heart?—clench. Protectiveness swept through him, so strong that he caught his breath. This feeling had more significance than jokes about Sir Lancelot and damsels in distress hinted at; he had a powerful urge to wrap his arms around Aubrey and never let her go, never let anything that was wicked or unpleasant touch her again. He needed to show her the magic. And so Robert drove on through the night....

AUBREY WOKE UP when the car stopped. At first she couldn't move. Her body, her neck in particular, was terribly cramped from her having lain in one position for a few hours. She licked her dry lips, blinked her eyes a few times and looked out the window.

The darkness had lifted, replaced by the cool, deceptive light of the false dawn. Directly out her window was a man-high wall of gray boulders. As she lay motionless, she thought she could hear a faint, rushing sound, then a small, ragged "boom." The sea, she thought. They had to be parked by the ocean, and the boulders were part of a seawall.

Her neck was beginning to object strenuously to its strained position, so she slowly lifted her head and stretched her arms and legs. Merlin, asleep on her lap, made a cat's sound of disgruntlement but didn't stir.

"Good morning," Robert whispered.

Aubrey carefully turned toward him. She was still a little dazed from sleep and disorientation, and that, she decided, was why Robert looked so good to her. He shouldn't, of course, look good at all after working all day and driving all night. But his eyes were bright and clear and shining, his smile wide and warm, and even the reddish stubble on his jaw and cheeks only added to his overall attractiveness. As for her, she didn't even want to think about how she looked.

She turned away from him, brought the seat back up, soothed Merlin, now awake, and mumbled, "Good morning."

Robert bit back a comment about this obviously being a particularly tough morning after. Instead he said, "You're just in time to see the sun rise."

She looked out her window again. Because of the wall, she couldn't see the horizon, but even the few clouds higher in the sky were beginning to glow pink. "Where are we?" she asked.

"New Hampshire."

"Is this where we were headed?"

"Nope." She looked back over her shoulder at him, both brows raised in question. "We've got just a little farther to go." He opened his door. "Come on. And bring my jacket, would you?"

He was at the top of the seawall and starting down the other side by the time Aubrey had pulled herself together, gotten out of the car—managing to keep Merlin inside—and shaken out his rather wrinkled and abused jacket. London Fog probably hadn't meant their stylish windbreaker to be used so disrespectfully, she thought ruefully, then followed Robert.

From the top of the wall she could see large, sloping rocks leading disjointedly to the ocean. The waves slapped against the rocks almost playfully, compared to the ocean's violence in the winter and its laziness in the summer. The rocks followed the ocean around to the left, but to the right was a large beach, lined farther down with many tightly packed summer houses. Aubrey gazed at the empty beach for a moment, wondering how crowded it would get in the summer, then looked straight ahead. There was nothing but water, without even a lobster boat to come between the land and the distant horizon and the magnificent spectacle of the sunrise.

She had made it just in time, for the clouds at the horizon were already on fire, glowing pink and red and gold, reflected in the pale blue water. Taking care as she climbed the rocks in her slick, leather-soled shoes, she made her way to Robert's side and draped the jacket around his shoulders. He smiled his thanks, then took her hand and looked back across the water. The red intensified, spread, then grew even brighter as the glowing sun eased above the horizon and took command. The sky and clouds and water had been setting the stage, and now the diva, the prima donna, had arrived. She rose swiftly, compared to all the preparations that had gone before, and Aubrey and Robert had to look away, for the full, still-red sun was too bright for them.

They remained, without speaking, for several more minutes. The morning seemed to come alive around them. Gulls and terns flew across the sky, gliding as, searching for breakfast, they turned their eyes to the rocks and water. A lobster boat, its engine shockingly loud in the still air, slid through the water. A jogger dressed in bright red appeared on the beach and ran just above the waterline, occasionally swerving to miss a foamy wave that washed up too high.

Following the dizzying flight of a tern with her eyes, Aubrey asked wistfully, "Are you sure we're not staying here?"

Robert put his arm around her shoulders and drew her close. "Don't worry. Where we're going is just as nice. And it's only about a half hour from here. You ready to go?"

She nodded and they walked back to the car, Robert helping her when her shoes threatened to slide out from under her. As they drove off, he told her that they were at Wallis Sands, a popular beach during the summer. They were going to drive back to Portsmouth, a wonderful resort town, then up Route 1 into Maine.

"Maine?" Aubrey repeated, visions of pine trees and rocky coasts and snow-covered mountains racing through her head. "I thought you said we didn't have far to go."

He looked at her with the patience of the seasoned traveler. "Maine's not in the Arctic Circle, you know. We're just going to southern Maine, right on the coast."

"But—"

"The New Hampshire coastline is only seventeen miles long, so how far could Maine be from here?"

"Seventeen miles?" She tried to picture a map of northern New England in her mind. She couldn't, having been no farther north than Boston, so she simply shrugged and watched the passing scenery.

There were houses set back from the road, small grocery stores and restaurants. The road took them into Portsmouth through the back door, so to speak, and Aubrey stared in fascination at the large New England clapboard houses: white paint and black shutters, railed porches and widow's walks and turrets. As they continued through the town, Robert promised that they would come back to sightsee and shop.

Then they were across the old drawbridge and entering Maine. Despite the early hour and a lack of restful sleep, Aubrey could feel her excitement growing. Even Merlin was taking notice, standing on her lap and bracing his front legs against the door as he gazed out the window, meowing occasionally at something they passed.

Not far into Maine, Robert turned off Route 1. "I'm going to take you in the long way," he said. "The scenery's great. We can visit the town of York later."

He was right. The road was narrow and twisting, like all good New England roads. There were modern homes built along it, but once in a while they would pass a private drive, and Aubrey could just glimpse a grand old house through the trees. Sometimes the road would dip, and the ocean would suddenly appear on their right, sparkling in the clear sunshine and beckoning to the far horizon. They passed a dirt road with a cluster of eight or more mailboxes at the head of it. Aubrey twisted to peer down the road but could see nothing; she almost asked Robert to turn around and go back. They passed a quiet cove, protected by encircling rocks and watched over by a house that appeared to be almost all glass, sitting on a cliff high above the ocean. When they came upon a charming stone church with a bell in the steeple, Robert slowed down.

"Here we are," he said, and turned right into a drive that was flanked by a low stone wall.

"Here we are where?" Aubrey asked, looking with interest at the winding asphalt road and the scrubby pine trees lining it. "Isn't this a private drive?"

"Nope."

Some small, connected white buildings appeared on the left. Cliff House Garage, the sign on one of them read. The road turned slightly to the right, and Robert pointed ahead of them. Aubrey gasped.

The magnificent building stood proud and alone at the top of the cliff. The cliff itself was surrounded on three sides—north, east and south—by water, a limitless, ageless view. Motel-like structures had been built into the sides of the cliff to the east and south, but Robert parked in front of the old inn, so that Aubrey scarcely glanced at the newer buildings. The inn was three stories high, white wood with a shingle roof, and a veranda ran along the front and eastern sides. Pillars rising two stories stood on either side of the front door.

Robert shut off the engine and turned to Aubrey. "Well?" he asked. "What do you think?"

She looked at him, her eyes wide with surprise and delight. "We're staying here?" He nodded. "Oh, Robert, I love it." Impulsively she leaned forward and threw her arms around his neck for a quick hug. "What a wonderful place for a vacation."

He held her to him and felt the last bit of tension ease from his body. He had feared she would be put off by the inn's obvious isolation, especially at this time of year. After all, she was used to the bright lights and excitement of Manhattan.

"I'm glad you like it," he said, his mouth close to her ear. He felt a shudder ripple through her body, and she began to pull away from him. He only let her go a tiny bit, though, just enough so that he could kiss her. He was careful, his lips only brushing hers; he didn't want to scratch her with his beard. She didn't respond at first, but then her lips softened and clung to his hungrily.

He gently put her away from him, brushing her hair back with one hand. "I know it's not very chivalrous of me," he said, his voice husky, "but I've got to get some sleep. Can we pick up on this later?"

She grinned. "Sure. And perhaps we could choose a better setting."

They put Merlin back in his cat carrier, despite his strenuous objections, and carried their luggage and the cat and his paraphernalia into the inn.

If Aubrey had been delighted with the exterior of the inn, she was enchanted by the interior. The front foyer was narrow but tall, a staircase on the right leading to the second and third floors. There were a fireplace and a large round mirror, wooden chairs that could be wheeled onto the veranda, and an elegant rug of faded roses. Doors off either side of the foyer led, she presumed, to bedrooms.

Robert looked around. "I hope someone's here. I called yesterday—"

The front door opened behind them, and a woman stepped inside. She was perhaps in her late fifties, with dark hair that had been sprinkled with sea salt. She was wearing a man's brown cardigan over a flower print cotton shirt and dungarees.

"You must be Mr. Browning," she said. "Sorry I wasn't here t' greet you, but I didn't expect you so early, and I was just mixin' up some biscuits when I heard the car drive up."

Robert seemed uncertain how to respond to this speech at first. He smiled and held out his right hand. "Yes, I'm Robert Browning," he said. The woman shook his hand heartily. "And this is Aubrey Jones."

Aubrey also shook the woman's hand, not at all surprised at its firmness or the calluses.

"And I'm Nan Waite," the woman said. "I'm in charge of the place right now. I've got your rooms ready, if you'd like to see them."

"Oh, yes," Aubrey said.

Nan picked up one of the suitcases and started up the stairs. Aubrey and Robert exchanged glances and shrugs, then picked up the remainder of their belongings and followed.

"I put you both together on the second floor," Nan said as she reached the second-floor landing. "But if you'd like to be elsewhere, just let me know." She opened a door and gestured inside. "You can share a bathroom or each use your own. It makes no matter mind to me."

Well, it made a matter mind to *her*, Aubrey thought. How dared Robert put them together in one room? She glared at him, then turned to Nan Waite to request another room. The older woman forestalled her, though.

"See how you like this room, Miss Jones," she said. "I prefer this southern view myself. You can see the light in the lighthouse at night."

Puzzled, Aubrey stepped into the room, but before she could start looking around, she heard Nan say to Robert, "And I thought you might like the other corner room, Mr. Browning," and she led Robert farther down the hall.

Oh, Aubrey thought, her righteous indignation evaporating. When the woman had said they would be together on the second floor, she hadn't meant in the same room. Aubrey would have to apologize to Robert for that dirty look she'd given him. Her mind at ease, she glanced around the room, and loved it immediately. The furniture was wood—a narrow double bed, a desk and chair, a lowboy—all painted a cream color with a delicate design of blue flowers. There was a small closet and, beside it, a sink with double faucets and a glass towel rack with cream-colored towels on it. The room had two windows, one looking east, the other south, and another door. She was just about to open it when she saw the knob turn. Nan Waite appeared.

"Now as I said," she went on to both Aubrey and Robert, who was behind her, "if you don't want to share the bathroom, one of you can use the one across the hall. It's all right with me. Everything okay in here, Miss Jones?"

"It's lovely, Ms Waite. Really lovely."

The woman smiled, emphasizing the well-worn laugh lines at the corners of her eyes. "Glad you like it. And call me Nan."

"If you'll call me Aubrey."

"And Robert."

An angry yowl from inside the cat carrier interrupted them. Aubrey laughed. "And Merlin," she said.

Nan left soon afterward, telling them to stop by her house, the first one to the left of the inn, after they'd rested. Aubrey and Robert listened to her heavy footsteps going down the stairs, across the foyer, and outside, then simultaneously sat down on Aubrey's bed.

"I'm exhausted," Robert said.

"Hmm," Aubrey said.

"Do you like your room?"

"Oh, yes. How about yours?"

"Very nice, like this except the furniture's gray."

"Hmm."

They sat in silence for a minute or two, and despite their tiredness, a tension began to build between them. Except for Nan Waite in a house a hundred yards away, they were alone. For a week, Aubrey thought. Sharing a bathroom. If Robert was planning a seduction, he couldn't have picked a better setting. She looked around the charming room, her gaze lingering on a bouquet of dried wildflowers on the lowboy, which Merlin was investigating. When Aubrey turned to Robert, she discovered he was looking at her.

"I don't suppose you want to nap together?" he said, his voice low, his eyes filled with tenderness and gentle teasing.

She shook her head.

"I didn't think so." He sighed. "Do you need to use the bathroom, or should I go first?"

"Well, I thought," she said hesitantly, "one of us could use the other bathroom."

He shook his head and gave her a chiding look. "And make extra work for that nice lady? I don't think it would be that much of a hardship to share a bathroom for a week. After all, you and Maggie do it all the time."

Aubrey refrained from pointing out that she and Maggie were both women, and that sharing a bathroom wasn't a hardship, per se. She simply wasn't sure she could comfortably luxuriate in a bubble bath when she knew he was only a closed door away.

"All right," she finally said. "We can share. And you go ahead. I want to unpack a few things."

He nodded and left, closing the bathroom door behind him. Aubrey began riffling through her suitcase, curious to see what Maggie had packed for her and trying to forget that Robert was just next door. She found a nightshirt and laid it out on the bed. She was in the midst of taking off her blouse when Robert tapped on the door.

"All done in here!" he called.

"All—all right," she answered, then sighed and released her stranglehold on the open shirt. *You would think*, she scolded herself, *that you were a high-school girl who'd never seen a man before, much less been near one.* Robert, she was sure, wouldn't have such a skittish reaction if she knocked on his door while he was taking off his pants. He'd probably tell her to come in!

"It's only a vacation," she mumbled as she pulled the nightshirt over her head. "Just enjoy it. And stay out of trouble!"

After quickly using the bathroom she slipped into bed, between the crisp cotton sheets, drew the blankets up to her neck and snuggled into the pillows. As she fell asleep she thought she heard Robert say, "Pleasant dreams, Aubrey," but decided she'd just imagined it.

6

"I'M IMPRESSED," Robert said when Aubrey joined him on the veranda around two that afternoon. She was wearing teal-blue cords and a red scoop-necked sweater with a butterflies-and-flowers design in clear-colored beads. Her hair was hidden beneath a black beret. She certainly didn't look as though she'd spent the night in a car.

Aubrey was rather impressed with Robert. She admired the red-gold highlights the sun brought out in his hair and the clean line of his jaw. He was wearing a doeskin-colored chamois shirt that emphasized his broad, strong shoulders. His jeans were beautifully faded, and she guessed from the cut and design that they were Calvin Kleins. She sighed unwittingly. Nothing looked quite so good on a man as a pair of faded Calvin Kleins.

Robert chuckled at her unabashed scrutiny of him. "Shall we head into town and find some lunch?" he asked.

She nodded. "Although I'd guess our chances of finding a restaurant open are slim."

The drive to York was brief, no more than five minutes. It was, Aubrey quickly saw, a typical but nonetheless attractive resort town. There were a beach and a huge parking lot. Small stores that probably sold everything from expensive clothing to cheap souvenirs in the tourist season vied with several motels for space. She was particularly taken with two hotels, prominently situated, that must have been around since the turn of the century: the Union Bluff Hotel, grandly set apart, with two turrets and an immense front porch; and the long and sprawling Ocean House, opposite the beach.

"What it must have been like to live here sixty or seventy years ago," Aubrey said, trying to picture the hotels as they would have been in their glory, patronized by the wealthy and well-dressed of Boston, maybe even New York.

Robert smiled at her. "There's even more of the romantic in you than I thought." He parked the car in front of a closed store on the main street. "Shall we try to find some food?"

They discovered one restaurant half a block away, on a side street, that was open. It was small, with dark wood tables and booths, hanging plants and pictures of such heartthrobs as James Dean, the young Marlon Brando and Elvis Presley. Two men were sitting in one booth, but otherwise the place was empty.

"Just sit down anywhere," a waitress said as Robert and Aubrey stood indecisively inside the door.

"You're still open?" Robert asked.

"Oh, sure. No problem. I'll bring you menus in a minute."

They chose a booth at the front, by the window that looked out over the quiet street. They had seen only a few people so far. Despite the bright sun and warm weather, Aubrey thought, the town had the feel of a resort in the dead of winter.

The waitress, a perky young woman wearing a jean skirt almost as short as her apron, brought them menus and water, then coffee when they both requested it. It didn't take them long to decide what to eat. They both ordered clam chowder, then a turkey sandwich for Aubrey and a roast-beef sandwich for Robert.

Silence fell between them as they sipped their coffee. Aubrey felt unnaturally shy and couldn't think of a thing to say. She blamed it on her system being out of whack from the long drive and the sleep, but when Robert took her hand and she jumped, she knew that wasn't the problem.

He looked at her speculatively for a long moment, then squeezed her hand and let it go. "Relax, Aubrey," he said in a low voice. "This is your vacation, and you don't have to do anything you don't want to do. You don't even have to spend any time with me the entire week if you don't want to. Of course—" a smile lingered "—I'd prefer that you did spend some time with me. After all—"

"What do you want from me?" she interrupted, leaning across the table toward him.

Something flickered deep in his eyes, a sweet tenderness that was gone before Aubrey could be certain it had been there. In its place was a mild friendliness, a casualness that she instantly distrusted.

"Your friendship, Aubrey," he said. "I ask for nothing more than that. As far as this week goes, I just want us both to relax, enjoy ourselves, spend some time together and get to know each other. No pressure, no expectations. Just friends."

"Why go to so much effort to just spend some time together?"

He laughed. "Frankly, I think it would be more effort to try to spend *any* time with you in New York. Between your schedule and mine—"

"Here you go, folks," the waitress interrupted them. "Two chowders, a turkey on rye and a roast beef on whole wheat. Anything else you need?"

"More coffee," Aubrey said absently, staring at her sandwich.

"Me, too," Robert said, and the waitress nodded and left.

"Look at this sandwich, Robert," Aubrey whispered. "It's lunch *and* dinner. I'll never be able to finish it." She measured it with her thumb and forefinger. "I'm not even sure I can get it in my mouth."

He critically surveyed his own sandwich, just as huge. "All this for two ninety-five," he said.

They both concentrated on their food, and since neither of them had eaten since the night before, it wasn't surprising that they both finished the chowder and every bite of their sandwiches. When she was through, Aubrey looked at the empty dishes in amazement.

"I can't believe I ate the whole thing," she muttered.

"I can't either," Robert said. "Do you eat like that all the time?"

"No. Actually, I'm pretty careless when it comes to feeding myself. I'll go to work and realize I've forgotten to eat dinner, so I'll have someone sneak me some food." She cupped her coffee mug in her hands and leaned her elbows on the table. "Cooking for one is pretty boring—" Robert nodded "—and I'm too cheap to eat out much of the time, so I just sort of ignore food."

"What would you do if you had someone else to cook for?" he asked, again with that casualness she didn't trust.

"I'd let him cook, particularly if he was into well-balanced meals. You know, a protein, a starch and a vegetable, all color coordinated."

He laughed. "Just like Mom used to make."

She shook her head. "Not like my mom used to make." She set her mug down. "Excuse me, I need to use the bathroom."

He watched as she walked to the back of the restaurant. He sensed again that her childhood hadn't been as happy as she had insisted. What *had* it been like, he wondered. When had her parents told her she was adopted? She had said that being abandoned by her natural mother had happened too long ago to matter, but he doubted she was being completely honest.

What, he wanted to ask her, had brought her to New York, so far away from her home? Life as an artist would have to be easier in the southwest than in New York, albeit less prestigious. And why did she seem so unsettled, as if she could pull up stakes any moment and move on, even though she had lived in the same apartment for six years? Was there anything in her life that she allowed herself to care deeply enough about to keep her in one place?

AUBREY LET THE WARM WATER run over her hands; they felt frozen. What was she going to do about Robert? He may have said he only wanted to get to know her better while on this vacation, but she knew he wanted more than that. He wanted more than any man she had ever dated. If she gave in, what would happen when he realized she was only interested in a brief relationship? What would happen if they became lovers, then she left him?

Or he might leave her.... An old hurt began throbbing within her at that thought, but she ruthlessly suppressed it, refusing to examine it. She turned the water off and quickly dried her hands.

When she came back to the table, Robert had already paid the bill and was ready to leave. As they walked outside, he suggested a stroll along the beach, and she agreed. The beach was large, at least by New England standards, and there were only a few other people on it. An elderly couple was walking a dog, a woman was sketching and a young couple was— Aubrey looked away hurriedly. A young couple was passionately kissing.

"Don't worry," Robert murmured. "I don't think we're disturbing them. I don't think a platoon of marines would disturb them. Although," he added, "it does give me ideas."

He took her hand, and Aubrey's entire body trembled. She was shaken enough by her conflicting emotional responses to Robert. Right now, she didn't think she could deal with her very straightforward physical response to him.

"I wonder how cold the water is," she said, her voice a little too loud, and tugged her hand from his and hurried to the water's edge.

Robert didn't follow her but simply stood still and watched. He knew she was puzzled by this whole situation, uncertain about what to expect from him. She couldn't run from him now and hide in her frenetic but emotionally undemanding life-style, but he would have to give her the space and time to figure things out for herself. Yet, he thought as her laugh danced on the air as she nimbly evaded a persistent wave, it wasn't going to be easy just sitting back and waiting. It had been a long time since a woman had touched his heart as Aubrey had, and she hadn't even been trying. How he longed to take her in his arms and make love to her, truly make love, but he wouldn't until she was ready. Until he knew their lovemaking would forge a bond between them that would not easily be broken.

"That water's freezing," she called, running back to him. "Do people really swim in it?"

He smiled at her, delighting in her sparkling eyes and flushed cheeks. "It warms up enough by the end of July or so. But Maine isn't like Jersey, you know, where you'll melt or get heat stroke if you don't jump into the water every half hour."

"Pity," she said. "I love swimming in the ocean."

"That sounds odd, coming from a land-locked New Mexico native."

"Ah, but I live in New York now."

"Why did you leave New Mexico?" he asked suddenly, then silently cursed himself. He'd no sooner vowed to give her time than he was pushing her to trust him, to be more intimate with him.

She didn't seem to take offense at his question. She merely shrugged, looking out over the water. "Why not? I'd lived there for twenty-two years. It seemed like time to go someplace else."

"Do you think you'll ever move back there?"

"No. I've got rather attached to New York."

He moved to stand in front of her, so that she had to look at him. "What does New York have that New Mexico doesn't have?"

He thought he saw irritation flash in her eyes at his persistence. "Fishing for compliments, Robert?" she said lightly.

He shook his head. "No. Fishing for you. I did say I wanted to get to know you better this week."

She opened her mouth, closed it, then finally spoke. "I just like New York better. There's more going on there, more variety of people, more different things to do, more . . ." She shrugged.

"Magic?" he said softly.

This time he definitely saw the irritation in her eyes as she took a step back from him. "Why do you keep bringing up magic? I'm not a child, Robert, who claps her hands because she believes in fairies."

"There are different kinds of magic."

"Such as?"

"The magic of a spring morning, of a newborn baby. Of what happens between a man and a woman when they touch."

He touched her, lightly. He put his hands on her shoulders and drew her to him. She held herself stiffly;

then he felt her melt slightly as his lips brushed her temple. He stepped closer to her so that their bodies were touching, and she didn't resist him. Encouraged, he let his lips trail down her face, her neck, back up to her ear. He felt her shiver and enfolded her in his arms.

She lifted her face to his, blindly searching for his mouth. His lips brushed hers once, twice, a third time. In frustration she caught his face in her hands and pressed her mouth firmly to his, her tongue tracing his lips, urging them to part. They did, and she gasped as a fire suddenly blazed within her when their tongues met. His hands moved feverishly up and down her back. Then one arm banded around her waist, pulling her hips tightly against his. They both moaned at the welcome pressure, and Robert plunged his tongue into her mouth, exploring it thoroughly, drinking in all of her sweetness.

"Magic," he murmured as his mouth left hers and traveled down her neck.

Her head fell back, and her eyes fluttered open. Something was wrong with the sky, she thought vaguely, but too enraptured by the feel of Robert's lips against her sensitive throat, she couldn't figure out for long moments exactly what it was. When she did, she swallowed and tapped Robert on the back.

"Uh, Robert," she said.

"Hmm?" He was too intrigued by the curve from her neck to her shoulder to pay much attention.

"I think we're about to be interrupted."

He lifted his head to look around, half-expecting to see some outraged elderly ladies bearing down on them, crying out that such indecent behavior was not permitted on this beach. He saw no one and turned back to Aubrey, puzzled.

"Look up," she suggested, her lips twitching slightly in an effort not to smile.

He looked up, and his eyes widened. Where minutes earlier there had been a gentle blue sky, there was now a huge, ferocious, thundering black cloud. The cloud was moving swiftly, covering the entire area, and Robert knew they'd have to run for shelter to avoid getting drenched.

"Come on," he said, taking Aubrey's hand and turning toward town.

She didn't budge. "Where do you want to go?" she asked.

He looked back at her in exasperation. "Aubrey, that—" he pointed upward "—is a rain cloud. They have a habit of blowing up very quickly along the coast and dropping torrential rain. I, for one, would prefer to remain dry."

"Why?" she asked, childlike.

"Aubrey..." He started to walk away, tugging on her hand, but she still wouldn't move. He glanced at her over his shoulder and saw that she was grinning.

"I love the rain, Robert," she said.

At that instant the rain began. There were no drops of warning. It simply came all at once, heavy and inescapable. Aubrey laughed, partly from delight with the rain, partly at the expression of astonishment on Robert's face. She wondered if he'd ever allowed himself to get caught in the rain.

"It's fabulous!" she cried, spreading her arms wide and spinning around, her face lifted to the sky.

He watched her in wonder, fascinated by her joy, by her obviously not caring that she—that they—were getting soaked to the skin. When she faced him again, her eyes bright, her smile wide, he suddenly began to laugh. She was right. The rain was wonderful. Standing in the midst of it instead of hiding from it, enjoying it without worrying about being caught without an umbrella, was wonderful.

"There you go, Robert," she said, laughing with him. "I knew you weren't that much of a stick-in-the-mud."

"If Gene Kelly can do it," he declared, "so can I."

She looked at him questioningly. He took her in his arms again and began dancing as he sang "Singin' in the Rain." She joined in, and for several minutes they danced across the wet sand while the rain poured over them, enclosing them in their own world of laughter and pleasure.

As abruptly as it had begun, the rain stopped. Robert and Aubrey were caught in midnote and midstride, and the quiet and calmness startled them. Aubrey looked up and was surprised to see that already the rain cloud was over the ocean. The sun and a few white clouds were again above the couple.

"Well, that was quick," she said, a bit disappointed.

"Too quick," Robert agreed. "I was just getting into the swing of it."

She laughed. "You were great. We'll rid you of your stuffy lawyer's demeanor in no time."

"I'm not stuffy! Although," he added somewhat sheepishly, "if you told any of my colleagues that I'd just danced in the rain on a deserted beach, they'd think I'd undergone a radical personality change."

"Thought so," she said smugly, then turned to gaze out over the water. "Oh, Robert. Look."

He looked, and smiled when he saw the rainbow rising over the ocean. It shimmered in the moist air, its red and green and blue arches seeming at first ethereal, then solid enough to be touched and held.

"See," Aubrey said softly, "if you don't outlast the storm, you miss the rainbow."

"The rainbow after the storm," he said musingly. "Or better yet, the magic after the storm."

He glanced down at her, but her gaze remained fixed on the already fading rainbow. Yet after a moment she murmured, "Yes. The magic after the storm."

THAT EVENING AFTER DINNER, Robert and Aubrey said good-night to Nan Waite and stepped out into the cool spring air.

"I can't remember when I've eaten so much in one day," Aubrey said, pressing a hand against her full stomach.

Robert chuckled. "Me, neither. But I think the apple pie was well worth any middle-of-the-night stomachaches." He paused. "Would you like to go right back to the inn, or sit out and enjoy the night for a little while?"

"Oh, let's enjoy the night."

They walked away from Nan's, down to one of the newer, motel-like buildings that looked directly out onto the ocean. It was enclosed by a porch, and they settled themselves on the railing.

"There's the lighthouse," Aubrey said, pointing straight out.

For a minute all Robert could see was blackness over the water, made even darker by the lights of town, just to the right. Then a bright point of light appeared, lasted perhaps fifteen seconds and flashed off again.

"Do you think lighthouses are romantic?" he asked.

"Absolutely. Most everything about the sea is."

"How about that?" He pointed farther out to sea, toward the east.

She turned and smiled at the sight of an almost full moon shining midway up in the sky, eclipsing the stars nearest to it. Those celestial pieces of silver cast a faint glow over the water, and for a moment Aubrey held her breath, sensing the magic in the air. Or perhaps, she thought as Robert's arm slid round her waist, the magic was in the man beside her. Perhaps he was the one to show the magic to her.

The thought startled her, and she instantly rejected it. She wouldn't make Robert out to be more than he was. He was just a man; there was no such thing as magic.

At least so she told herself, but when Robert turned his head so that his warm breath wafted across her cheek, followed by his lips, she wasn't so sure.

"You should see yourself in the moonlight," he whispered. "Moonbeams are dancing in your hair, and all of you seems to be ethereal."

She shivered, partly from the night air, but mostly from his evocative words and voice. How could she ever have thought him a stuffy lawyer? And how could she ever have thought any other man was romantic?

Feeling her shiver, Robert tightened his hold. His own words surprised him; he'd never even thought of saying anything like that to a woman before. Perhaps something in the air tonight was bringing out the romantic in him. But no, he knew what it was—Aubrey, a woman unlike any he'd ever known. Without thinking about what he was doing, never heeding his plans to take things slowly and easily for a few days, he allowed his lips to explore her face, her smooth cheek, the faint hollow at her temple, the vulnerable corner of her mouth.

She trembled but didn't pull away, and with one hand he turned her face toward his. The moon and stars were the only illumination, and in that light her face was filled with intriguing shadows. Her eyes were half closed. He slowly lowered his head to brush her parted lips with his own. She sighed and relaxed against him, her arms encircling his neck, and he pressed his mouth firmly to hers. Their tongues sought each other's, entwined, spoke without words. When her tongue slipped into his mouth, he moaned.

She was lost, Aubrey thought, somewhere out at sea without even a lighthouse for guidance. But she didn't care. All of her suspicion, skepticism and hesitation were swept away in the glory of Robert's embrace, his kiss. When his hand left her face and trailed down her body, lingering at her neck, nudging aside her shirt so that it could cup her shoulder, then continued on to skim her breast, she instinctively shifted on the narrow rail, offering herself to his touch.

As he caressed her, his thumb circling then rubbing against her firm nipple, she broke their kiss and nibbled on his neck, his ear, stroked with her tongue the part of his chest bared by his shirt.

"Aubrey." His arm tightened around her waist, and his hand dropped to her thigh. "We shouldn't—I said... I promised we would wait."

Wait, she thought. Wait for what? She frowned and looked at him.

He sighed, tempted by both the desire and frustration he saw on her face to throw his good intentions to the winds. But he wouldn't. He had to be sure.

"Aubrey," he said, cupping her face in his hands, "I said at lunch today that we should get to know each other better." He smiled wryly. "Our bodies are getting along just fine, but we need to share our minds . . . and hearts."

She pulled away and looked out toward the water. She had been right. Robert did want more from her than any other man had. Her mind and her heart. Her instinctive reaction was to say no, to be evasive, to walk away. But something held her there, some strong emotion that had been sparked by this man, that grew whenever he was near. She couldn't walk away, not right now.

"What—" she began, but her voice broke, and she had to try again. "Did you have something specific in mind that you'd like to know about?" she asked.

Robert stared at her, nonplussed. This was neither the time nor the place, nor even the manner in which he'd expected to share confidences and life stories with Aubrey. But if she was willing . . .

"Tell me about your childhood," he said softly.

She shot him a quick glance of surprise. How had he known her family life hadn't been exactly what she had pretended it to be? She was silent for a minute, wondering what to say, then murmured, "It wasn't all a bed of roses."

"No childhood is."

"It's particularly true for adopted children. We're insecure because our natural parents didn't want us and insecure because we're constantly afraid our new parents will give us back."

She paused. "That's not to say that my parents ever threatened me with that, ever purposely made me insecure. But it wasn't a . . . stable household at the best of times."

Her voice was low and tight; Robert could feel the tension in her body. Obviously, she found it difficult to reveal herself.

"Both my parents were artists, my mother a painter, my father a potter and jewelry maker. They traveled a lot to get new ideas for their work. Sometimes they'd take me with them; sometimes they wouldn't. The house, when they were home, was constantly filled with artist friends and freeloaders. People would stay for a few days, a few weeks, then leave and come back months later."

Robert was beginning to understand. The environment that had helped forge Aubrey's character at a young age was coming clear. "Has anyone ever stayed for you?" he asked.

She looked at him, and in the dim light he could see her brows draw together in a frown. "What do you mean, stayed *for* me?"

He gently pushed her hair back, his hand lingering on her cheek. "Has anyone ever loved you enough to stay with you? Loved you so much that he wouldn't, couldn't, leave you?"

She drew back from him, and he thought he saw a glimmer of tears in her eyes. "My parents love me!" she said, her voice harsh with emotion.

"There are varying degrees of love. From what you've said—and haven't said—I would guess you've loved many people, but they haven't loved you as strongly in return."

Aubrey drew in her breath sharply. How could Robert see so clearly into her heart, so unerringly point out the cause of much of the hurt and disillusionment in her life? For a moment she was tempted, tempted to lean her head against his chest and let him, like a noble knight, protect her. She was tempted to give up her heart to him, to let the love bottled up inside her flow out, flow over him. Then the old fear rose again, reminding her of earlier, painful partings, of her vow to remain uninvolved so as to avoid that pain.

"Trust me, Aubrey," Robert was whispering. "I won't leave you like that."

She wanted to, longed to believe him. But she was too afraid. Years of habit and self-defense were too much to overcome. "No," she murmured, shaking her head as she slid off the rail. "No, I c-can't."

Her voice cracked on the last word, and she ran away, up the hill to the inn, leaving Robert alone in the moonlight.

7

AUBREY AWOKE THE NEXT MORNING to the sound of whistling. For a minute she was disoriented, not certain where the whistling was coming from. She glanced around the room but didn't see Robert. Rolling onto her side, she looked at the bathroom door. Open!

"Robert!" she croaked, then swallowed and tried again. "Robert! What are you doing? Why is the bathroom door open?"

"Good morning, Aubrey," he called cheerfully. "Lovely day. I hope I didn't wake you, but the bathroom was so steamy after my shower that I had to open the doors to clear off the mirror so I could shave."

It took Aubrey a minute to work through all that; then she buried her face in her pillow. "How can you shave and whistle at the same time?" she mumbled.

"What, Aubrey? I didn't hear you."

As he spoke, his voice came closer, accompanied by footsteps. Aubrey's shoulders stiffened under the blankets as all her senses reported that Robert was standing right beside her bed.

"Aubrey," he said softly, "you'll suffocate if you fall asleep like that."

She couldn't help smiling, and pushed herself over onto her back to look up at him. Her breathing stopped instantly. From the hips up, Robert was naked. His hair was still damp from his shower, lying sleekly against his head. She knew she shouldn't look, but she couldn't keep her gaze from drifting downward, over an intriguing dusting of red-gold hair to a lean waist and flat stomach. A towel, thankfully large, was wrapped around his hips, but below that Aubrey could imagine strong, well-shaped legs with the same red-gold hair. To make sure, she would have to peer over the edge of the bed, and she had a bit more dignity than that. Reluctantly she pulled her gaze back up to his face, unwaveringly meeting the amusement in his eyes.

"Good morning," he said again, his voice oddly husky. "Sleep well?"

She nodded, then looked away from him. "Uh, Robert . . . about last night . . ."

He seemed to tense, but his voice was casual when he said, "What about last night?"

"I . . . did a little thinking before I fell asleep."

He sat down quite naturally on the edge of the bed, his hip pressing against her thigh. For a moment she lost her train of thought, mesmerized by the sight and feel of such intimate parts of their bodies so close together on a bed.

"You did some thinking . . ." he prompted, and she quickly looked up at him.

"Yes, and . . . you were right, Robert. No one's ever really loved me that—that strongly. But I'm not self-pitying about it," she added hurriedly. "I guess I got used to it."

"And learned to protect yourself."

She nodded, and her gaze dropped from his. "Yes. I don't . . . commit myself to anything, to anyone."

With one hand under her chin, he lifted her head so that she was looking at him. "What about me, Aubrey?" he asked, his voice low. "I'm committed to you."

Her breath caught. The warmth in his eyes seemed to touch her physically; the tenderness in his voice caressed her. How could she resist him? How could she not try, once more, to love?

Her hand cupped his cheek, and she smiled tremulously. "I'll try, Robert. I can't promise any more, but I'll try."

His smile wasn't in the least tremulous. It was dazzling, so happy that she could believe for a moment that everything was going to work out. He turned his head to kiss her palm, then grinned at her.

"I'm glad, Aubrey. And this certainly was unexpected. I really just came in here to wish you a proper good-morning."

"Proper?"

He settled his hands on either side of her, bending near her in slow motion. "Proper," he murmured, his face close enough so that his breath wafted across her mouth.

She swallowed, unexpectedly nervous, then grimaced. Robert's breath was tinged with peppermint toothpaste. Hers certainly wasn't. She pressed one hand against his chest, shocked for a moment at the wonderful feel of his bare, warm skin, and turned her head away.

"Morning breath," she muttered, trying not to breathe on him.

He turned her head back with one knuckle against her chin. "I don't care."

She covered her mouth with her hand. "I do."

He kissed her hand, then traced each finger with his tongue, his gaze locking with hers. "It's just like eating onions," he said, then sucked for a moment on her little finger. When her eyes fluttered closed with pleasure, he smiled. "Once you kiss, it doesn't matter."

His mouth left her fingers and explored across her cheek to her hairline, then blew her hair away to find her ear. She inhaled sharply when his tongue gently outlined her ear, and her back arched slightly. Her brain sent out a token protest—this was too volatile and suggestive a situation—but she firmly told her mind to quit being sensible, and let herself simply feel. Her cocoon of blankets had been comfortably warm but was now growing surprisingly hot, and she was tempted to toss back the covers. Robert's forearm was pressing against the side of her breast, and her nipples were beginning to harden, aching for some attention. She tangled her fingers in the hair at the back of his neck and urged his mouth closer.

"What about your morning breath?" he asked, his lips brushing hers tantalizingly.

"What morning breath?" she whispered, and pressed her mouth firmly against his.

As their tongues met and caressed and stroked, Robert slid his arms around her body, pulling her to him. Her breasts were crushed against his chest, and he moaned into her mouth. She drew her legs up and pressed them against him, frustrated by the barrier of cloth between them, aware that all of her body was eager for his touch. Wrapping her arms around him, she leaned back into the pillows, taking him with her.

He followed gladly, intoxicated by the feel of her warm body beneath him, the sensuous movements of her hips and legs. He wanted to do nothing less than strip the blankets from her and plunge into her, to sink deeper and deeper into her warmth, to make her his. One hand cupped her breast, squeezed it, his fingers teasing the erect nipple. Not satisfied with touching her through the soft nightshirt, he skimmed his hand down her body, pushing the blankets to her thighs, then started back up along her bare flesh, slipping under the nightshirt. When he reached her naked hip, he stopped. Aubrey tore her mouth from his and drew in a ragged breath as she pressed her hips upward in an instinctive invitation.

Robert groaned and lowered his head to her shoulder, his breath hot against her skin. "Aubrey," he said, his voice harsh with suppressed desire, "we have to stop."

She was silent and motionless for a minute. Then her arms dropped to the bed, releasing him. "All right," she said, her voice amazingly light.

He lifted his head and stared at her. "All right?" he repeated. A wry grin quirked one corner of his mouth. "You're not even going to try to talk me out of it?"

"Nope," she said, her eyes twinkling as she teased him. Then she grew somber. "Robert—" she stroked his smooth cheek "—I'm glad you stopped us. My body may be ready to make love to you, but my mind still isn't."

He sat up. "I know. I'll try not to rush you." He grinned wickedly. "But I won't promise that I won't try to persuade you."

She smiled. "That's fine. I like your brand of persuasion."

He dropped a quick kiss on her forehead and stood up. "Now that that's settled, I suggest you shower, dress and meet me on the veranda for breakfast in twenty minutes."

"Twenty minutes!" she exclaimed. "It'll take me that long to shower. And isn't it too cold to eat outside?"

"Twenty-five minutes, then, and no, it isn't." He winked and disappeared into the bathroom; a few seconds later she heard his door to the bathroom close.

She stretched luxuriously, groaning slightly when she heard some bones in her back and neck crack. She wasted a few minutes of her allotted time remembering the delicious weight of Robert's body on hers, his arousing kiss, his hand on her bare hip like a brand, marking her as his.

"My dear girl," she murmured, "what are you getting yourself into?" Then she bounded from the bed and hurried into the bathroom.

BREAKFAST WAS HOT SCONES with butter, and coffee laced with cream and cinnamon. The sun burned clear and bright in the spring sky, creating a wide stream of silver water in the ocean, stretching from the rocks to the horizon. After they were through eating, they drove north to Ogunquit.

Ogunquit was much like York, though perhaps a little more upscale. "This place is overrun with tourists in the summer," Robert said as he parked the car in Perkin's Cove, the shopping district of the small town. "York is a little more sedate, which is why I prefer it."

"How do you know so much about Maine?" Aubrey asked as they got out of the car.

"My family used to vacation up here a lot when I was a kid."

"Was this where you'd been when we met three weeks ago?" Three weeks ago, she repeated to herself. Was that all the time they'd known each other?

"No," he said. "I'd been visiting a friend in Boston. How about you?"

"Oh, I hadn't been anywhere in particular. I just felt the need to get away, so I took the weekend off, packed a bag and Merlin and started driving. It was a nice break."

They had walked down to the water, and the salty breeze off the ocean was blowing Aubrey's hair behind her like a black flag. She closed her eyes and lifted her face into the wind, smiling slightly. Robert was struck again by her strong beauty—and by her intriguing mysteriousness.

"Want to take a walk?" he asked.

She opened her eyes and turned to him, still smiling. It was a smile of such pleasure and peace that he ached to take her in his arms and love her, so that she would smile like that for him. "Walk where?" she asked.

"By the ocean, of course." He took her arm and led her toward the water and a wide path that ran along it. "It's called Marginal Way and follows the ocean for about a mile."

"Sounds lovely."

They walked in silence at first, admiring the restless, dark blue ocean and the surrounding cliffs. Benches were interspersed along the path. After they'd gone about a quarter of the way, Robert sat down on a bench and beckoned Aubrey to join him.

"This is really nice," she said, stretching out her long legs and tapping the toes of her sneakers together.

"Mmm," he answered, closing his eyes and leaning back to let the sun warm his face.

She studied him for a minute, then asked, "You really love it up here, don't you?"

He opened one eye and looked at her. "What could possibly make you think that?"

She laughed. "So what are you doing in New York? I mean, you really seem more like the country type."

He sat up and shrugged. "I happen to have a job in New York."

"I'm sure you're a perfectly competent lawyer who could get a job someplace else."

"A job in my father's firm," he added.

"Oh! I didn't know that. Your father's a lawyer? Why didn't you tell me that?"

He smiled. "Hadn't gotten around to it yet, I guess."

She was suddenly struck by the desire to know everything about Robert. She turned to him eagerly. "What else haven't you told me?"

"Well, let's see. I told you I have a younger brother and two younger sisters. And that we raised champion collies." She nodded. "Did I tell you that I traveled through Europe the summer after college and before law school?"

"No. Where did you go? Was it wonderful? I've never been to Europe, but I'd like to go."

He stroked her cheek, amused by her childlike enthusiasm. How different from the wary woman who worked at Alex's. "You'd love Europe," he said. "Especially all the traveling around. It would make the Gypsy in you happy." Something flickered in her eyes, and she started to turn away, but he stopped her. "Don't shut me out, Aubrey. Talk to me. A relationship is a two-way street, you know."

She stood abruptly. "Don't push me, Robert. Give me time."

He reined in his frustration and stood, as well. "Come on." He took her hand. "Let's keep walking."

Again they walked in silence, a slight tension between them. Aubrey stared out to the far horizon and wondered what to do. She knew Robert was right, that a relationship was a two-way street, that she had to give if she expected him to give. Still she held back, and she wasn't even sure why. What, she asked herself, was she afraid of? No answer was forthcoming, from the ocean or the gulls or herself.

Sensing Aubrey's confusion and distress, Robert set out to cheer her up. He told her about the wonderful summer house his family had rented every year, about how he and his brother would dare each other to be the first into the cold ocean in early June. He told her about learning how to kiss one night when he was thirteen, instructed by a fourteen-year-old girl who worked at the soda fountain, and how for the rest of the summer he spent every afternoon at the soda fountain—until her fifteen-year-old boyfriend suggested he make himself scarce.

"Whatever happened to her?" Aubrey asked.

Robert sighed. "Alas, I never spoke to her again. The next few summers I had a job, so if I came up here at all it was only for a week or two."

"Pity."

"Why?"

She stopped walking and grinned cheekily at him. "I'd like to thank her for teaching you such marvelous technique."

"Oh, you would, would you?" he said, walking toward her slowly.

"Yes, indeed," she said, giggling as she backed away. "I believe in giving credit where credit is due."

"Uh-huh." He quickened his pace. "And I don't deserve any credit?"

"You were just the raw material she was working with. Like a sculptor and a lump of clay."

"That does it!" he roared, and charged her.

She laughed and started running, surprising him with her swiftness and her ability to avoid his grasp. She reached the end of the path, and before her stretched seemingly endless miles of beach.

"Uh-oh," she muttered as her feet hit the sand, "no place to hide."

Robert was only a few paces behind her, and she hadn't gotten far along the beach before he grabbed her and tumbled with her into the soft sand, landing on top of her.

She laughed up at him in between pants for breath. "That ought to have worked up an appetite," she said.

"I'll say." He shifted his hips, pressing lightly against her, letting her know he was thinking of a different kind of appetite. He enjoyed her little gasp of surprise. "But before we . . . satisfy ourselves, there's a little matter about giving credit where credit is due that we should settle."

"Oh?" She tried to hide her laugher, but it bubbled up anyhow, making her shake and increasing her awareness of Robert's body lying heavily on top of hers.

"Yes," he said. "Tell me how claylike this seems to you." He lowered his head swiftly and captured her mouth.

She didn't put up a fight but wholeheartedly joined in, parting her lips to the thrust of his tongue. Her fingers wove through his hair, and she pressed his head closer, kissing him with more passion than she ever had before. He groaned, and one of his hands slid down her body, stopping at the outer swell of her breast. She arched her back, pushing her hips against his and giving him access to her tingling flesh. He cupped her breast, his thumb rubbing across her nipple, teasing it to an erotic hardness.

His touch enflamed her, and again she thrust upward, her eager body telling him how much she wanted him. He shifted, pulling away from her slightly so that his hand could slip between them and unbutton her blouse. The cool air on her flesh was a tantalizing contrast to the heat of his hand as he caressed her naked breast.

"You're so wonderful, Aubrey. So wonderful," he murmured as his mouth left hers, traveled down her neck. He ran his tongue around her breast, flicking its rosy crest, then finally took her into his mouth. She gasped and again held his head to her, offering herself, aching for more of his fiery touch, more of his love.

Again he shifted, lifting his hips from hers, and she moaned her disappointment. Then his hand was on her belly her hip, then cupping the hot, moist center of her. As she cried out his name, a part of his brain reminded him they were on a public beach. But the taste, the feel of her was so intoxicating that he told himself, *Just a little more. A little more...*

Her hands were under his knit shirt, pushing it up, running up and down his back. When his bare chest touched hers, he wanted to melt into her, never to be parted from her. He kissed her once more, his tongue entering her mouth with undeniable demand and intent. She responded wildly, wrapping her legs around him as if to weld him to her.

The shocking intimacy of their position struck them both at the same instant, and their bodies tensed, motionless. Robert pulled back and stared down at Aubrey. She lifted her lids slowly, and he was pleased to see her eyes glazed with passion.

"Aubrey," he said, his voice strained, "this really isn't the place."

She managed a small smile. "No, I guess it isn't."

He quickly kissed her, then buttoned her shirt. "Later," he promised before smiling a teasing smile. "After dinner."

"After dinner!" she protested as he lifted himself off her and stood up. "Why not now?"

He helped her up and dusted the sand from her back. "I have plans for this evening."

"With whom?" she snapped.

"You, silly. Besides—" he took her hand and started walking back to the path "—haven't you heard that anticipation makes the fruit all the sweeter?"

"If you don't starve first!" she retorted, glaring at him. Why was it, she wondered, that despite her best efforts, Robert remained fully in control of this relationship?

BACK AT THE INN, Robert told her to be ready to leave by three-thirty and to wear something nice. Since it was only one-thirty, Aubrey decided to take a nap. She set her alarm clock and curled up on her bed in the sun with Merlin, and quickly fell asleep. When the alarm sounded, she turned it off, buried her face in the pillow and went back to sleep. The loss of the sun was what finally woke her, for she'd grown chilly. She looked at her clock, then bolted from the bed, ignoring Merlin's cry. It was three-ten. How could she ever get ready in twenty minutes?

She flew across the room to the closet and flung open the door. She couldn't remember for a moment what Maggie had packed for her that was nice, then groaned when she saw the dress hanging there. Actually, it was Maggie's dress, but she'd given it to Aubrey several weeks earlier, saying it was too tight on her. It was black, naturally, and made of a linen and rayon blend— "It doesn't wrinkle . . . much," Maggie had promised. It was perfectly respectable in the front, with a high collar and a very straight, simple cut. *Or make that a form-fitting cut,* Aubrey thought, eyeing the dress dubiously. The front didn't really worry her, and neither did the slits on either side of the narrow skirt. It was the back of the dress that made her hesitate; it didn't begin until almost the waist.

She flung the dress over the bed, then pulled its saving grace from the closet, a dark blue and silver Oriental silk jacket that would keep her both warm and decent. She added to the pile the black-patterned stockings and high-heeled midnight-blue sandals Maggie had provided. "You'd think that woman wanted to get me into trouble," Aubrey muttered, casting an uncertain glance at the ensemble.

Apparently Robert was dressing, for he didn't answer her knock on the bathroom door. She slipped inside, splashed cold water on her face, then confronted her makeup bag. Knowing Maggie, Aubrey assumed she had added a few surprises; Aubrey herself hadn't bothered with makeup since they'd arrived in Maine. She took a deep breath, peeked inside the bag then groaned again. She should have known. All that was left of her regular makeup was her blush and lipstick. Her subtle eye shadows, liner and mascara were gone, replaced by glittery, nighttime makeup. There were blue eyeliner and mascara, sparkling eye shadows in pink and gold and copper and blue. The translucent face powder she used occasionally was also gone, in its place a powder that gave her face a golden shine, particularly in dim, romantic lighting.

When Aubrey was done applying the makeup, she had to admit Maggie had not done her a disservice. The exotic shadow emphasized her eyes, which she considered her best feature, and the powder did give her face an attractive glow. Aubrey stared at her mirrored reflection and smiled with the awareness of her feminine power and confidence. She still didn't know what she wanted from this relationship with Robert, but there was nothing wrong with looking fabulous while she made up her mind. Glancing at her watch, she saw she only had three minutes left and hurried back to her bedroom.

She was dropping the dress over her head at the same time that she was slipping her feet into the sandals, when a knock sounded on the door.

"In a minute!" she called, her voice muffled by the dress. Concentrating as she was on getting ready, she didn't hear the door open, didn't realize that Robert was in the room, until she had the dress over her hips and heard a low whistle. She whirled, almost falling off the unstrapped sandals.

"I said in a minute, not come in," she said to Robert. She wasn't sure, however, if she was more irritated with him for invading her privacy, or for seeing her before she was completely ready and could stun him with a planned entrance.

"Sorry," he said, his smile indicating he wasn't sorry in the least.

"Hmph," she replied, and turned to the mirror over the lowboy, gathering her hair into her hands.

"Don't put it up," he said quickly, taking a few steps toward her as if to stop her bodily. Their eyes met in the mirror, and she looked at him questioningly. He shrugged. "I like it better down. Besides," he added, teasing, "you might need it to keep from catching cold."

"I do have a jacket," she informed him, and deftly swirled her hair into a French twist and began sticking hairpins in it. When she was through, she looked at him once more in the mirror, smiling slightly. He returned the smile, knowing she'd bested him. Now he'd spend the entire evening staring at her hair, wanting to free it, to let it fall over her naked shoulders, to run his hands through it....

He cleared his throat and straightened. "Ready to go?" he asked.

She shook her head, enjoying his discomfort. For now she had him in her power, and she was going to savor this moment.

She lifted one leg, rested her foot against the chair in front of the desk and leaned over to fasten the shoe. Because of the slit in her dress, she figured Robert was getting a good view of most of her leg. When she was done with that shoe, she switched legs, careful not to look at Robert. She straightened and smoothed her hands over her hips, making it seem like an unconscious movement, then turned her back to Robert, again facing the mirror. From her jewelry case she took dangling jet earrings and fastened them in her ears, admiring for a moment their effect—and Robert's fascinated gaze. She then took from the case three slender bracelets made of mother-of-pearl, and slipped them on. They'd clink against themselves all evening, she knew, reminding Robert of when she'd put them on.

Last was her perfume. She picked up the small bottle, tipped it and carefully applied the stopper to the insides of her wrists and elbows, then behind her ears. She regretted for a moment the high neck of the dress, which kept her from putting perfume at her throat and between her breasts, but noting Robert's hot gaze, she figured perhaps it was just as well. Maggie had provided a sparkling evening bag with a long strap, and Aubrey carefully filled it with a lacy handkerchief, some money and her lipstick. She then turned to Robert and gestured to the jacket on her bed. With a smile he held the jacket out for her, and when she slipped into it, his hands closed briefly around her shoulders and pulled her lightly against him.

"Are you sure you want to go out?" he murmured, his lips against her temple.

For a moment she allowed herself to relax, to enjoy the feel of his strong body, his hands surprisingly warm even through the padded shoulders of her jacket, his voice low and husky and full of promise. She was tempted to say no, that she didn't want to go out, but then remembered his earlier frustrating comment about anticipation. This would teach him.

"You don't think I did all this just for you, do you?" she said, slipping from his light hold. "Your job for the evening is to show me off."

"Ah." He nodded. "Glad you explained that. I was thinking of getting dinner at a drive-through McDonald's and then going to a drive-in movie." Desire flickered in his eyes. "I'm not sure I want to share you."

"It's not sharing," she said, slipping the strap of her bag over her shoulder and walking to the door. "It's . . . showing off."

He followed her without answering, too busy admiring her swaying walk in the high heels; the way the little bag carelessly hit against her hip; her lush, restrained hair. Anticipation was one thing, he thought, but this just might kill him.

8

"NOW WILL YOU TELL ME where we're going?" Aubrey asked. They were in her car, Robert driving, following the winding asphalt drive from the inn to the main road.

He grinned. "Maybe."

"Wherever it is, is there food there?"

"Why, of course."

"Is it far?"

"Closer than New York."

"We're not really going to a drive-in movie, are we?"

"Don't you like movies?"

"Movies are fine. It's the drive-in part I don't care for."

"Had a bad experience once, huh?"

"Actually, more like three or four times. I was a slow learner."

Robert laughed. "What happened?"

"Not much, which of course didn't make the guy too happy. He just didn't realize that I really liked those B-grade monster movies they show at drive-ins and that I wanted to watch the movie."

"How old were you?" She didn't answer, turning away to look out the side window. "Aubrey," he persisted, "how old were you?"

She said something, but in such a quiet voice he couldn't understand her.

"You want to try that again?"

"Fourteen."

He shot her a look of astonishment. "You were fourteen! And going out with a guy old enough to drive a car! What did your parents think of this?"

"They didn't know."

He gave her a few more speculative glances, then shook his head and chuckled. "I don't see why any of this surprises me. You're obviously not the type to do anything in an accepted, middle-class way."

She laughed wryly. "That's putting it politely. I wasn't a real hard-core rebel when I was younger. I just didn't like following rules, doing what was supposedly right for me."

"Like dating boys your own age."

"Mm. Among other things."

"You probably smoked."

"Yep."

"Cut classes in high school."

"And college."

"Wore jeans that were too tight and had patches all over them."

"Of course."

"Partied all the time and still managed to pull straight As."

"Well," she said modestly, "there were a few Bs every now and again."

"My kind of woman."

"Uh-huh. But are you my kind of man? What were you like in high school and college?"

"You're not going to like this. In high school I was shy and incredibly studious. I was on the chess team, took all advanced courses, studied on Friday and Saturday nights. Etcetera, etcetera."

"Oh, boy. No sports even?"

"Just tennis."

"Just tennis? Why do I get the feeling it was more than just tennis?"

He shrugged. "Well, we were state champs my junior and senior year."

She groaned. "While I was forging doctor's excuses to get out of gym class, you were mopping up on the tennis courts. It figures. How about college?"

He turned and grinned at her. "Oh, in college I really broke out. I gave up studying on Saturday nights, at least."

She clapped her hands twice. "Congratulations. What did you do instead?"

"Had orgies."

"I'm sure."

"Actually, in all seriousness, I did go a little wild in college. I was still obnoxiously studious, but I also realized there was a little more to life than getting on the dean's list."

"Such as?"

"Playing in a jazz band."

She twisted in her seat to look at him, her eyes wide. "You're kidding! What instrument?"

"The clarinet." He smiled, pleasantly reminiscing. "That band was just a little bit different than the band and orchestra I played in in high school."

"I'll bet. Did you perform often?"

"About every other Saturday night at the local beer joint on campus. Sometimes we'd play at one of the bars in town; sometimes we were hired to play at parties on campus."

Aubrey was intrigued by this new aspect of Robert. "I wish I'd known you then. I can just picture you on stage, wailing away on the clarinet. Do you ever play now?"

"Only for myself. And—" he inclined his head toward her "—anyone else who cares to listen."

She smiled. "I'd love to sometime." She fell silent for a minute, thinking. "You know, Robert," she said slowly, "I probably know some people who might like to meet a clarinetist."

"Oh, yeah? Women, I hope."

"Idiot." She punched him lightly on the arm. "No, musicians. I know some jazz musicians. Maybe you could join them for jazz sessions or even a gig every now and then."

"Sounds good." He smiled. "I knew it was my lucky night when I met you."

A SHORT WHILE LATER they arrived in Portsmouth, New Hampshire.

"It's only in the past ten years or so," Robert said as he drove slowly through the town, "that Portsmouth has really started looking out for itself. There's been a lot of reconstruction, upscale businesses and restaurants moving in. It's a popular place with the tourists."

"Looks like a nice place to live," Aubrey said, admiring the brick buildings and the few brick sidewalks, the attractive cleanliness and smallness of the town. "A little different from New York."

"Just a little." He looked at her thoughtfully as he stopped for a red light. "I'm not sure you'd be content here for very long."

Anticipating a comment about her life-style, Aubrey braced herself. "Oh?" she said a bit coolly. "Why not?"

"Even if you were raised in the quiet of the southwest, you do prefer the excitement of the big city. The opportunities, the chance to try something different as often as you'd like."

Well, that wasn't so bad, she thought. "The chance to try something different." That was a nice way to phrase her inability to stick with something . . . or someone. She covered her eyes with her hand as she felt a pang of fear. She wanted so much to be with Robert, but what if she discovered that she truly wasn't able to commit herself? What if she hurt him?

"Aubrey? Aubrey, what's wrong?"

She dropped her hand into her lap and opened her eyes. They were sitting in a parking lot. Robert was turned toward her, looking at her with concern.

"Don't you feel well?" he asked.

"I just . . . have a headache. It happens sometimes when I take naps in the middle of the afternoon. Throws my system off or something." She smiled reassuringly and patted his hand. "I'll be all right. I probably just need some fresh air."

"Well, we do have to walk across the street to the theater."

"Theater?" She looked around. "That's the theater?"

He chuckled. "That's it. It used to be a warehouse."

He helped her out of the car, and they walked across the street to the Theater by the Sea. The lobby, filled with people wearing everything from silk to denim, was mostly glass. On display were many pieces of beautiful, innovative pottery. Aubrey eyed with interest and longing one particular plate, then glanced at the card beneath it to check the price.

She gasped. "And I thought New York was expensive," she muttered to Robert.

He grinned. "Would you like a drink?" he asked, gesturing to a small bar on the other side of the lobby.

She shook her head. "Not right now, thanks."

"Let's get our seats, then."

He led her to the entrance to the house, and smiled when her eyes widened in astonishment. The house would have been the main part of the warehouse, and was a deep but narrow space. Seats rose in steep tiers from the front of the theater up to where Robert and Aubrey were standing. The walls were whitewashed plaster, and she couldn't decide if the atmosphere was rustic or very modern.

A woman took their tickets, after which an usher led them to their seats, down in front and in the center. "How did you get such great seats on such short notice for a weekend performance?" Aubrey whispered to Robert.

"Just lucky."

She looked disbelievingly at him.

"All right," he admitted. "I know one of the actors."

"Are you *sure* you don't live here and not in New York?"

"Actually, I met Daniel in college, and he used to live in New York. Moved up here almost two years ago."

"Oh. And he got you the tickets?"

"Right."

Aubrey nodded, satisfied, and turned to her program. The show for the evening was Oscar Wilde's *Lady Windermere's Fan*. Lover of Victoriana that she was, she had read the play but had never seen it performed.

"Is your friend in the play?" she asked, searching the cast list for a Daniel.

"No, but his sister-in-law is." He pointed to the name opposite the Lady Windermere role: Toni Burns Townsend.

"Theatrical family," Aubrey said.

"Daniel's wife, Chris, used to be a costume designer in New York, then chucked it all to come up here and manage a restaurant."

"From costume design to running a restaurant. That's quite a switch."

He shrugged. "No more than from painting to bartending."

She shot him a quick glance. What did he mean by that?

He caught her eye and turned slightly in his seat to face her. "I wasn't being judgmental with that remark, Aubrey. Far from it. Chris was miserable in New York, even doing something she loved, so she came here for a change. She was lucky enough to find so easily something, and someplace, that could make her happy.

There's no law that says you have to settle down with one job in one place by a certain time."

Aubrey stared at him, trying to understand what he was saying. What she saw in herself as an inability to commit he saw as an inability fo find her niche, a desire to "try something different," as he'd said in the car. Could he be right, at least partly? Or did he not understand the extent of her waywardness?

"Robert," she said, "I didn't just go from painting to bartending. There were eight or nine other jobs in between."

He smiled. "Somehow that doesn't surprise me. How many roommates?"

She blinked. He was certainly taking this all well. "Uh, I'm not sure. Six, maybe."

"Boyfriends?"

She lifted her chin slightly. "That's an awfully personal question."

"I know."

He waited, and she finally said, "Dozens. But only— let's see—two serious ones."

"In six years?"

"No, since I started dating when I was fourteen."

He mused on that for a moment, then asked, "How serious?"

"Robert! Really!"

The house lights flickered, then started to go down.

"How long did they last?" he whispered, leaning close to her.

"More than a month, less than a year," she whispered back.

"Was either of them your lover?"

The lights started coming up on stage.

"Hush," Aubrey said, mindful of the people sitting around them. The house was full.

"Were they?" Robert repeated.

"Yes," she hissed, then refused to say any more.

The play began with Lord Darlington, a bachelor who was quite attracted to Lady Windermere, calling on the lady in question, a young married woman. After Lord Darlington left, Lord Windermere arrived. He tried to convince his wife to invite a Mrs. Erlynne to her upcoming birthday party, a woman with a less-than-sterling reputation. Lady Windermere refused, believing her husband was having an affair with the woman. He wasn't, and he also knew that Mrs. Erlynne was his wife's mother. She had run off with her lover, abandoning her infant daughter. Aubrey had forgotten that part of the story, and she frowned, feeling vaguely uncomfortable.

As if sensing that, Robert reached over and held her hand.

Throughout the rest of the play, Aubrey found her attention torn between the fine performance on stage and her rambling thoughts about her life. As though Robert's persistent questions about her earlier boyfriends had unlocked some door deep in her mind, memories of all the boys and men she'd dated over the past fourteen years tumbled through her brain. The memories were brief, like images flashed on a screen, but telling. With the exception of two men, she'd never been serious about anyone. All the others had been filler. She'd just been waiting for the right man.

Aubrey lightly grasped Robert's hand in the darkened theater, listening to Lord Darlington, disappointed in love by Lady Windermere's rejection of him, avow that, "We are all in the gutter, but some of us are looking at the stars." Aubrey knew then that she was ready to take that next step with Robert. Maybe it wouldn't work, maybe she would run from him in the end, but for now she wanted him...needed him. He was the best man she had ever known, and she wanted to share everything she was with him.

"DID YOU ENJOY THE PLAY?" Robert asked as they left the theater.

"Oh, yes," Aubrey said, thinking more of the decision she had come to than what had been enacted on stage. "Your friend's sister-in-law is quite good," she added absently.

"Yes, she is," Robert said, looking at Aubrey curiously, as if aware of her preoccupation and wondering what had caused it. "Ready for dinner?"

She flashed him a smile. "Absolutely. Will that be in a warehouse, too?"

He smiled mysteriously. "You'll see."

They drove only a short way to get to the restaurant, but Portsmouth was a small town. Robert parked on a narrow street in an obviously residential district and led Aubrey to an old wooden church.

She cocked her head up at him. "We're eating in a soup kitchen?" she asked.

"Not bloody likely," he replied, pretending to be offended. "This is one of the classiest restaurants north of Boston."

She looked at the sign above the door. "With one of the oddest names. Seventy-two? Or is that just the address?"

"It was the address. The restaurant used to be on Islington Street, back there—" he gestured behind him "—the main street through town—although, of course, farther uptown it's called Congress Street and then becomes Daniel Street."

"Of course," Aubrey murmured.

"And," Robert went on, giving her a stern look, "it was number seventy-two, so they named the restaurant Seventy-two Islington."

"Uh-*huh*. And when they moved into the church and off Islington Street, they trimmed the name down to just Seventy-two."

"You catch on quick."

She gave him a haughty look, then turned pointedly toward the door. With a courtly bow, he opened the door and gestured for her to go in. He ruined the effect, though, by pinching her as he followed closely behind. She would have scolded him, but she was too astonished by the interior of the restaurant.

You couldn't go anywhere but up. Staircases on the right and left curved to the second floor. Glancing over her shoulder at Robert, Aubrey quickly climbed the one on the right. She found herself at the front of the dining room and what must have been the main sanctuary when the building had been a church. As the maître d' approached them and spoke to Robert, Aubrey gazed unabashedly around the restaurant.

Everything was dark wood and cream and shades of red. The carpet was rose, as was the pressed-tin ceiling. The tablecloths were white linen, accented by burgundy-colored napkins, and on each table was a small lamp that gave a feeling of intimacy and seclusion. The walls were papered in cream and rose, and arched windows stretching from the chair rail almost to the ceiling were topped by stained glass. The curtains were the same cream color as the wallpaper.

As she automatically followed the maître d' to their table, Aubrey noticed that at the front of the restaurant what would once have been the choir loft was now a small cocktail lounge.

"Oh, Robert," she said, turning to him as the maître d' pulled out her chair for her to sit down, "can we have a drink up there first?"

Robert and the maître d' exchanged amused glances; then Robert smiled at Aubrey. "Of course," he said. He nodded to the maître d' and escorted Aubrey up the stairs to the lounge. There were only a few people there. They sat on a plush sofa facing the back of the restaurant.

"This is beautiful, Robert," Aubrey said, impulsively taking his hand. "I don't think I've ever seen a more lovely or elegant restaurant. Look, they even have ceiling fans and chandeliers."

He brought her hand to his mouth and sweetly kissed it. "I'm glad you like it," he said. "It is lovely and elegant, but not as lovely and elegant as you."

Their eyes met and held, and Aubrey felt her hand begin to tremble in Robert's. If he kept looking at her and saying such wonderful things, she doubted they would make it through dinner.

"May I get you a drink?" a woman asked, and they both turned to see the bartender standing in front of them.

Thankful for the interruption, Aubrey slipped her hand from Robert's. "A Scotch and water, please," she said. "No ice."

"Scotch on the rocks," Robert said. "No water."

The bartender smiled, then left, and Robert turned to Aubrey. "Don't you know you're supposed to order something delicate and feminine," he said teasingly, "like white wine or a kir?"

She raised her brows and grinned. "You must be joking."

He sighed. "I guess I am. You're a lost cause."

She waved her right arm in the air, so that her bracelets clinked and chimed, and shook her head slightly to set her earrings dancing. "A lost cause, eh? Sorry to hear that."

"Unfortunately—" he grasped her right hand and again brought it to his lips "—I'm even more of a lost cause than you are, thanks to that little glimpse into the feminine world you gave me earlier." He kissed the back of her hand, then turned it over and kissed her palm. His thumb stroked her wrist where she had scented it with perfume, and his tongue slipped from between his lips to delicately taste her skin.

She gasped softly, then tugged to get her hand back. "Robert," she whispered, "not here."

He let her hand slide from his grasp, his eyes locked onto hers. "Just giving you a little glimpse into the masculine world, Aubrey."

The drinks arrived, and Aubrey was glad to be able to hide behind her Scotch. As she relaxed against the back of the sofa, she became aware of music playing. She looked around, wondering where it was coming from.

"Robert—" she began, but he knew what she was going to say, and pointed to the balcony at the other end of the restaurant.

"Over there," he said.

On the balcony was a three-piece band and two couples waltzing. The balcony was very small, and from where they sat, it didn't look to Aubrey as if one more person could fit on the dance floor.

"Would you like to dance?" Robert asked.

She looked at him warily. His voice had been casual, but there was a gleam in his eye, and his half smile dared her to refuse. Well, at least she had her jacket to protect her naked back. And this was a public place. She'd be perfectly safe.

"I'd love to dance. Do you think we should order our dinner first?"

"Good idea."

They picked up their drinks and walked back down to their table, which was set in one corner near a window. A waiter immediately brought them two menus. Aubrey read the menu longingly before leaning across the table to Robert.

"Do you think we can order one of everything?" she whispered.

After much debate and indecision, they finally settled on their choices. They would share an appetizer of chilled split lobster remoulade, then Aubrey would

have the swordfish pecan and Robert the tournedo with
shallots and cream sauce. After Robert gave the waiter
their order, he stood up.

"Shall we?"

She pushed back her chair, and he was immediately
beside her, helping her up. His hands were on her
shoulders, slipping beneath the collar of her jacket.

"You don't want to wear this while you're dancing,
do you?" he said. "It'll be too warm."

She started to protest, but he already had the jacket
halfway off her. Resignedly she slipped out of the
sleeves, and he draped it over the back of the chair.
Taking her hand, he led her up to the balcony, then took
her in his arms.

Aubrey had learned ballroom dancing in college and
had forever regretted it. She loved to dance and could
foxtrot like nobody's business, but she'd been spoiled
by the men in her class. Most of those she'd danced with
since knew only how to gyrate in the rock or disco style,
or in what she called the high-school-make-out style—
his arms wrapped tightly around her waist, his head
nestled between her neck and shoulder, his body barely
moving. But finally, she thought, as Robert began
leading her in a sedate waltz, she'd found a man who
could really dance. He let her right hand rest on his left,
not grasping it too tightly, while his right hand was
pressed firmly against her back, just at the ribs, exactly where it should be. She was so delighted with
Robert's ability that she forgot for a moment that that
right hand was pressed against her *bare* back.

"You're a good dancer," he said, smiling down at her.

"Only because I'm being led by a good dancer," she said.

"Thank you. Or rather, thank my mother. Or even more, thank Mrs. Johnston, the dance teacher. After all, she just took this lump of clay—"

She squeezed his hand. "Oh, hush. I was just teasing."

He chuckled. "I know." He tightened his arm and swung her around.

She followed him easily, standing on her toes to turn and allowing her body to lean against his for balance. Out of habit, she stared into his eyes; when waltzing and turning, staring into a partner's eyes was sometimes the only way to maintain a sense of balance. But when they finished the turn, she didn't look away from Robert, nor did he relax his hold on her. Slowly she became aware of his hand branding her naked skin, of his eyes burning into hers. She felt herself go weak with the knowledge of his desire for her, and with the realization that her own desire for him was growing by the moment. The tension between them seemed palpable, and his left hand actually trembled beneath hers. She leaned closer to him; at that moment the music ended, and Robert immediately stopped dancing. He didn't release her, though, and Aubrey took a deep breath, just to reassure herself that her body was still her own.

"This isn't quite the right dress to waltz in," she said, hoping to lighten the atmosphere and bring them both back to their senses.

He blinked and quickly glanced at her, from head to foot. "No," he said, then nodded toward another couple as the music started up again. "But great for the foxtrot."

She turned to look at the only other couple on the floor, an older man and woman doing an energetic foxtrot.

"Can you foxtrot?" she asked, looking coyly up at Robert.

"Can I foxtrot?" he repeated scoffingly. "Can a fish swim?"

He spun her once to get into the rhythm of the music, then easily flowed into the simple steps. It had been so long for Aubrey that she had to count out the first few measures, but it all came back to her quickly. As her body adjusted to Robert's lead and began following instinctively, she smiled up at him. "I always did like to foxtrot," she said.

"Obviously. You're quite good."

"Thank you. It's surprising, considering how little ballroom dancing I've done over the years."

"I'm surprised you even know it. No offense intended," he added quickly when he saw her eyes start to flash. "You just seem more like the fast-dancing, no-touching type."

"Well, I like that, too, but I took a ballroom-dancing class in college."

"What inspired that? Had a crush on the teacher?"

"You're just full of witty remarks tonight. Actually, the truth is even worse than that. I took it spring term during my senior year to fulfill my phys ed requirement."

Robert laughed. "I should have known." He paused. "But did you have a crush on the teacher?"

"No, though he may have had a crush on me. He would often ask me to help demonstrate a new step."

"Like how to turn a sedate, socially acceptable foxtrot into a rumba?"

Aubrey's eyes widened, and then she laughed. Robert was absolutely right. Although her feet were following the rigid pattern of the foxtrot—and incidentally the rumba—her hips had taken on the seductive sway of the rumba. "What can I say?" she said, shrugging. "Once he taught me this, the good, old-fashioned, foxtrot seemed kind of boring."

Robert laughed, as well. As the music wound to an end, he spun her so quickly that she had to clutch his shoulders to keep her balance. When he stopped, she was facing the older couple, and they both smiled at her.

"It's great seeing young people doing ballroom dancing," the man said to them. "Most people nowadays don't see the advantages to it." He winked at Robert, and Aubrey swallowed a giggle.

"Obviously you two have been dancing together for a long time," the woman added. "You move beautifully together."

"Thank you," Robert said, trying hard to keep a straight face. Aubrey, he noticed, had given up and had tucked her head down, hiding her face. As the older couple left the dance floor, he muttered, "You can look up now. They're gone."

She raised her head and grinned at him. "I'm sorry. It just all struck me as very funny for some reason. I mean, what a bawdy comment for that man to make.

And I don't think the woman realized her double entendre when she said we move beautifully together."

Robert raised his brows as he led her back to their table. "You, my dear Miss Jones, have a dirty mind. Either that or you're rather preoccupied with a certain subject. And why might that be?"

Realizing she was caught, Aubrey decided a brief retreat was in order. She picked up her bag and said, "I think I'll take a quick trip to the ladies' room to make sure that wild dancing hasn't ruined my hair."

He looked at her hair with disgust. "Don't worry. It didn't jar it in the least."

She smiled and patted his cheek. "Don't pout so. I'll be back in a minute."

SATIATED WITH GOOD FOOD AND DRINK, Robert and Aubrey stepped out into the night. It was chilly but clear, and Aubrey held her jacket closed around her as she and Robert walked to the car. While he unlocked her door, she gazed up at the sky. It was glittering with stars.

"A stargazer, huh?" Robert said, slipping his arm around her waist and pulling her close.

"Actually, I was thinking about Lord Darlington's line in the play, about us all being in the gutter and some of us—"

"Looking at the stars," Robert finished for her. "Yes, I was struck by that line, too." He put his hand behind her neck and eased her head down until she was looking directly into his eyes. "I know I'm looking at the stars all the time," he added, his voice low, his meaning clear.

"Are you?" she murmured. She moved so that her lips were barely a breath from his. "I guess I am, too. And I now know how to find my way around them."

"Oh?" His mouth brushed hers. "How's that?"

"I have a set of directions: 'second star to the right and straight on till morning.'"

"And where will that get you?"

"To never-never land. At least, according to Peter Pan it will. But I know an even better way to get there."

"Oh?"

"Take me back to Cliff House, and I'll show you."

9

THE DRIVE BACK TO YORK was quick and quiet. They held hands, Aubrey's resting on her leg, Robert's covering it. Occasionally she stroked his fingers; occasionally he explored her nylon-covered knee. Aubrey felt she might explode if he didn't touch her more intimately. She had to keep telling herself this was neither the time nor the place.

Robert parked in front of the inn, and they got out of the car. They walked slowly up the steps to the front door, down the hall to the stairs, up to the second floor. They stopped in front of her door.

"Would you like a few minutes to...uh...well, whatever?" Robert asked.

How sweet, Aubrey thought. Robert could be so assertive sometimes, then shy and tender at other times. She appreciated his thoughtfulness, but anticipation had brought her to a fever pitch already. She wasn't in the mood for waiting any longer. She took his hand, opened her door and led him inside.

The moon, just a shade less than full, was shining on the water and filling the room with a soft glow.

"Do you mind if we don't turn the light on?" she asked, almost whispering, reluctant to lose the romantic feel of the silent, moon-washed room.

"No." She could see his half smile. "It'll be bright enough come morning."

His words, and the image they invoked of them lying close together when the sun rose, raised her temperature another degree. She laid her bag down on the desk, then slipped her jacket off and threw it on the chair. He did the same with his jacket and tie, then held out his arms to her.

His body was hard and warm, and Aubrey melted against him. Never, she thought, had anything felt so good. His hands were firm and demanding on her back, pressing her to him, exploring her cool skin. He murmured her name as he nuzzled her neck, her ear, her cheek. Finally he found her mouth with his, and she sighed and leaned more heavily against him. With lips and tongues they learned each other, tasted each other, until they were both gasping. Robert grabbed her hips and pressed her to him, and they both moaned at the sweet frustration.

"Aubrey," he said, his voice raspy, "my mind says we should go slow, but my body's telling me it can't wait."

"Neither can I, Robert," she said softly.

Without conscious thought she began unbuttoning his shirt. He helped her pull it from his trousers, and when it was hanging open and free, she rubbed her face against his chest. Her arms slid around his waist, and she kissed his neck, loving the taste and scent and warmth of him. She felt a slight tugging at the back of her head and realized that he was pulling her hairpins out. They hit the wooden floor with soft pings, and then he was running his hands through her hair, smoothing it over her bare back, lifting it to his face and kissing it. Their eyes met, and her breath caught in her throat when she saw the passion in his expression, the incredibly sensual and potent smile on his beautiful mouth.

"You had your fun teasing me earlier," he said. "Now it's my turn."

He turned her and pushed her down so that she was sitting on the edge of the bed; then he knelt in front of her. He lifted one of her feet, and with a light, sensuous touch, unfastened the sandal and slid it off. The fingers of one hand caressed the sensitive arch of her foot, while his other hand slipped up the back of her calf. She gasped at the surprising eroticism of his caresses, and he smiled up at her. He repeated the process with her other foot. This time, though, both his hands slid up her legs, rounded her knees and inched under her tight skirt. Something hot began flowing through Aubrey's lower body, and she parted her legs slightly.

"Your stockings are wonderfully sexy," he murmured, dropping a kiss just above one of her knees, "but I'm afraid they'll have to go."

She nodded, mesmerized by his rich voice and glowing eyes, and lifted her hips. His hands reached up to her waist, found the elastic top of her pantyhose, and eased the hose off her. He murmured approval as he caressed her bare legs, then quickly disposed of her underpants, as well. He shifted so that he was kneeling between her legs, and Aubrey again thought that nothing had ever been this wonderful before. Never had a man loved her so carefully, with such intimacy, seeming to know exactly what would please her. He kissed one leg, his tongue sensuously licking her, and she trembled with longing.

"Cold, sweetheart?" he asked, pushing her dress higher up her legs so that he could kiss her thighs. "That is a rather drafty dress, isn't it?"

"Mmm," she murmured, her hand stroking through his hair, gently guiding his head over her tingling skin. "You're wearing more clothes than I am."

"Am I?" He stood, and she made a small sound of loss. "Can't have that." Quickly he shed his shirt, slipped off his shoes, unfastened his belt and trousers and pushed off the rest of his clothes. He cast them toward the corner of the room.

Aubrey's eyes widened at his sudden nakedness. Then she smiled with delight and admiration at the beauty of his splendid body. His shoulders and chest were broad, though he wasn't muscle-bound. His waist and hips were lean, his legs sturdy and long. His chest and arms and legs were dusted with hair that looked soft and appealing, and she reached out a hand to touch him. He obligingly knelt once more between her legs, and she stroked his body with something akin to wonder, her hands smoothing over his strong shoulders and down across his chest, pausing to tease his nipples, then slipping lower to his taut belly. Her legs reflexively tightened around him, sliding against his warm skin, drawing him closer to her.

"Keep that up," he warned, his hands slipping under her dress to cup her buttocks, "and I won't be able to wait."

"Keep *that* up," she said, arching her hips and gasping as the tips of his fingers brushed that most sensitive and aching part of her body, "and I won't want you to wait."

He smiled with satisfaction, and suddenly pulled her off the bed into his lap. His thighs were hard beneath hers, his arousal pressing intimately against her. She shifted, unconsciously entreating him to love her then and there, and he drew her head down to his for a passionate, almost bruising kiss. Their mouths were feverish, hungry for each other, and their hands explored the other's body without shyness or hesitation. Their breathing became labored, punctuated by moans of desire, until Robert finally pulled away.

"Your dress," he gasped.

She pulled it up over her head. Robert's hands were instantly on her breasts, fondling them, admiring their fullness and firmness. His tongue was soon exploring each nipple, bringing them to an almost painful hardness. With a cry, Aubrey pressed his head to her, offering herself to him, and he took one nipple into his mouth and sucked, biting lightly with his teeth, driving her mad with desire.

"Robert!" she cried.

He stood up, lifting her with him, then fell across the bed with her. His body was heavy on hers, but she welcomed the weight . . . welcomed him. He stared for a timeless moment into her eyes, brushing an errant lock of hair back from her face. Then with a gentle yet powerful surge of his hips, he entered her.

She gasped, her body arching, her hands clutching at his shoulders. For several seconds she remained motionless, absorbing the feel of him, his forcefulness and his tenderness. She trembled and slowly eased her hips back down to the bed.

"Are you all right?" he asked, the concern in his voice prompting her to open her eyes and look at him. "I didn't hurt you, did I?"

What a wonderful man, she thought, stroking his face and smiling. What a wonderful, wonderful man. She shook her head and said, "Oh, no, you didn't hurt me. Make love to me, Robert. Now. Please."

His answer was a strong thrust that took her breath away. She wrapped her arms and legs around him and gave herself up to him. Robert's body was all that was real to her, that and the wondrous, magnificent things it was doing to her, for her, the joyous rapture it was releasing within her. As the ecstasy grew within her, she held on to him more fiercely, moved more feverishly, striving for, reaching for, something. And then suddenly she was there, she found it, and she cried out as an ocean of sensation overwhelmed her, swept her away. Robert trembled above her, burying his face in her neck as his hips pounded against her, and she was tossed even higher into the stormy oblivion.

Their bodies stilled, and slowly their breathing quieted, their heartbeats returning to normal. Aubrey loosened her hold on Robert, and he lifted his head to look at her.

"Good thing this inn's sturdy," he said, smiling.

She laughed softly. "The bed, too."

"Am I too heavy?"

"Not yet."

They held each other without speaking for a few minutes; then Robert said, "Thank you."

"My pleasure."

"And mine." After a pause, he added, "We must do this again sometime."

"Like in an hour or so?"

He chuckled. "Or so. I'm not eighteen anymore." He explored her neck with warm lips and tongue, then kissed her mouth lingeringly. "Then again, I might be inspired...."

"Do you suppose we could slip under the covers first?"

He laughed, and they did.

As THE RAYS of the early-morning sun glided into the room, Robert awoke. For a moment he was confused, unsure if he was dreaming. Then he remembered the night, the lovemaking, the inexpressible joy and delight he had found in finally coming so close to Aubrey. She was snuggled against him, her back to his front. One of his arms was draped over her waist and pressed to her breasts, and she was loosely holding on to his wrist with both hands. Their legs were entwined, and her hips were nestled into his.

Sweet, Robert thought. Sweet and wonderful. As physically satisfying—to put it mildly—as their lovemaking had been, he had been overcome by the emotional impact of it. Never before had he felt so close to a woman, so open to her. Had Aubrey felt the same way? She wasn't one, he had discovered, for talking either during or after their loving, and yet there had been something in her tired, happy smile, something in the way she had stroked his cheek, that made him hope she had felt, had shared, that special closeness.

He tightened his arm around her and dropped a kiss on her head. But no matter how close they may have come during the night, he knew she didn't love him. He knew that as clearly as he knew he loved her. And because he loved her, he was willing, again, to wait, to wait until she'd come to terms with him, with her life, with her search for magic. For now, at least, he could bind her to him in the most elementary and pleasing way.

He slid his hand down her naked body, past her slightly rounded belly to the tangle of curls between her thighs. She stirred and mumbled but didn't waken. He caressed her gently, carefully, his touch obviously arousing her, for he felt her grow moist. He raised himself on one elbow and kissed her cheek, her jaw, her temple, then outlined her ear with his tongue while his fingers grew bolder. He could feel a slight stiffening in her body, then she gave a small cry and woke up.

"Robert." Her voice was breathless, already throaty with passion. She arched her back, seeking more pleasure from his delightful touch. Still groggy with sleep, she tried to figure out what was happening, to separate the various sensations running through her. Her ear was moist from Robert's kiss, and now he was nipping lightly at her neck. His body was hot and hard against hers, his arousal pressing against her buttocks. And in her lower body, a heavy pressure was growing, growing with each flick and caress and fondling of Robert's fingers. She groaned and clutched his arm, almost mindless with excitement, eager to have all that pressure explode into ecstasy and yet wanting the anticipation to go on and on.

Robert shifted, pulling her body half over his and holding on to her with his other arm. "Just let yourself go, Aubrey, love," he whispered. "Don't hold back. Don't be afraid."

Her hips began undulating, and his stroking quickened, hardened. The pressure within her continued to build until she thought she'd go mad, and then suddenly it all burst. Her body seemed to become liquid gold, without beginning or end, one with Robert. Tingling sensations went on and on, peaking then subsiding, only to peak again. She murmured Robert's name, dazed by his fabulous loving, and was barely aware of his arms around her, of his shifting her off him, of his rolling on top of her.

When he entered her, though, smoothly and easily, like one river flowing into another, her body became her own again, and she used it to please him, to bring him the joy he'd brought her. She lifted to meet his thrusts, moaning as her passion began to grow once more. When his movements quickened she clung to him, striving to reach the summit with him. And she did; they did, both crying out, their bodies trembling with the force of their love. Then they both collapsed, limp yet still shaking, holding on to each other.

After several minutes Robert rolled onto his back and cuddled her close to his side. He kissed her on the forehead, and she looked up at him.

"Good morning," he said.

"Umm," was all she could manage.

THE REMAINDER OF THEIR TIME in York passed sometimes quickly, sometimes slowly. Most mornings they didn't get out of bed until well after the sun had flooded Aubrey's room with warmth and light. After breakfast, which they had either in town or at Nan's, they would drive around the area—up the rocky coast along Route 1, inland to the mountains. One day they drove back down to Portsmouth, and Aubrey gladly spent a week's salary there, buying a wool skirt and sweater at half price, handcrafted wooden salad bowls, tiny brass Christmas-tree ornaments and for Robert a tweed cap. She said it made him look like a Scottish gent.

Toward the end of the week, the weather was warm enough for long walks on the beach, and on Friday they even had a picnic. Nan provided them with lobster rolls, potato salad and Boston cream pie for dessert. Robert added a bottle of wine. The sun was bright that day, the breeze off the ocean surprisingly mild, so they spread their blanket out in the middle of the beach.

When they had polished off the food and half the wine, Aubrey lay back on the blanket with a long sigh of contentment.

"Happy?" Robert asked.

"Mmm. Wonderful place."

"Better than New York?"

She opened one eye and squinted up at him. "Different, at least."

"Better than New Mexico?"

She didn't answer for a moment, then said, "Much different."

He sipped some wine. "You never did tell me why you left New Mexico."

She looked up at him. He was wearing the tweed cap, despite the warm sun, and a flannel shirt with the sleeves rolled up. Silhouetted against the blue sky, he looked strong and masculine. "It's no big mystery why I left New Mexico," she said. "I'd finished college and decided it was time to get out . . . to do what everyone else had been doing all my life."

Something in her voice, more sadness than bitterness, made him look sharply at her. "Did you leave alone?" he asked.

She threw an arm over her eyes. "Yes," she mumbled.

"But . . ."

She sat up abruptly and faced him. "For most of my senior year in college I lived with a guy. Andy. We were very much in love. He was my first lover."

Her voice lowered. "There was something poignantly romantic about the whole thing. We had a small apartment, a few pieces of secondhand furniture and very little money. We were terribly carefree, and I thought it would go on forever."

She looked away from Robert, out to sea, following the flight of a gull. "It didn't go on. He left after graduation. He said he wasn't ready to settle down. He bought a decrepit VW bug, packed, said he'd keep in touch and drove off. I left for New York two weeks later."

Robert was silent. It was a sad ending to a first love, true, but it had happened seven years ago. Yet Aubrey still carried the hurt with her, bolstered by her memories of all the other times she had been left behind. Small wonder she'd been so careful about not getting deeply involved, small wonder that, even now, she was so edgy with him. But did she fear more that he would leave her, or that he wouldn't?

THE MOON ON SATURDAY NIGHT was waning, just beyond full, and unselfishly cast its silver over everything—the ocean, the rocks, the trees, the lawn. Aubrey sat at the desk in front of the window, brushing her hair, contemplating the serenity around her.

It had been a good week. Yet as sorry as she would be to leave, she was eager to return to New York, her friends, Alex's. She was even eager to see how things would work out between her and Robert when they returned to the real world.

She knew it would be difficult. With their disparate schedules they would have little time to share. Her own life was so full that she wondered when she would fit Robert in. Or would he, now that he was her lover, demand more and more of her time, resenting her when she saw other friends, when she went away for a few days to be alone? She needed that space, she told herself firmly, those other contacts, those . . . those escape routes.

Oh, wonderful, she thought. What a great way to be committed to a man—by planning when and how often you could run away from him. How was this relationship ever going to work?

"I haven't the foggiest idea," she murmured, setting her brush down on the desk.

"Haven't the foggiest idea about what?" Robert asked, gently massaging her shoulders.

She jumped a little at his voice and touch. She hadn't heard him enter the room. "Nothing," she said. "Just thinking."

His hands tightened on her shoulders even as she recognized how automatically evasive her answer had been. This serious-relationship business, she thought, was not going to be easy.

She rubbed her cheek against one of his hands by way of apology. "We can talk about it later," she said. "Right now I've got other things on my mind."

"Oh?" he said, fingering the satin tie of her negligee. "And what could that be?"

She laughed and stood up, certain that she would appear almost luminescent in the dark room with the moonlight behind her. Robert caught his breath, and his gaze traveled slowly over her, from the lace-edged neckline of her gown to her bare feet. The thin, ivory-colored fabric hinted tantalizingly at her naked body, even as the low neck revealed the upper swells of her breasts and the slits at either side showed off her long legs.

"No," he said, his voice hoarse with passion, "I don't need to ask what's on your mind."

His hands came to rest lightly on her shoulders again, and he bent his head to kiss her. He seemed almost afraid to touch her at all, as if he'd lose control if he did. Aubrey wanted him to lose control, and as his tongue parted her lips she stepped closer to him and placed her hands on his waist. He was wearing only his jeans, faded and tight-fitting, and the feel of his warm, bare skin inflamed her. She was the one who was going to lose control, she realized, but she didn't care. She wrapped her arms around his back and pressed her body against his. His response was to crush her to him as his tongue thoroughly assaulted her mouth. Her breasts tingled with excitement as the satin and lace of her gown rubbed against them, keeping them from the bare skin of his hard chest. She moaned with frustration at the clothes that separated them as their hips pressed urgently together, eager for the final joining. Robert ran his tongue over her lips, soothing them, promising more. He pushed her head down onto his shoulders and held her tightly. His breathing was harsh, and she knew he was struggling with himself, trying to slow things down.

"Oh, Aubrey," he said, "what you do to me. No other woman has ever made me feel like you do. I've never felt for any woman what I feel for you." He dipped his head and kissed her quickly on the lips. "Aubrey, I love you."

He might as well have dropped her into the cold Atlantic. Her body stiffened, all thoughts of lovemaking gone, and she pulled away from him. For a timeless moment they stared at each other; then Aubrey slumped down into the chair.

How can he do this to me, she asked herself in despair. Just when she thought she could handle it all, he had to go drop another bomb. He loved her? Why? How could he? What did it mean?

"Aubrey." He dropped to the floor beside her and took one of her cold hands in both of his. "I didn't mean to stun you so, but I thought you should know."

That was pretty lame, he thought, anxiously studying the expression on her face, trying to decipher her feelings. Perhaps he shouldn't have told her, but it hadn't felt right not to. He believed in honesty, even if it caused more problems than it solved.

"Oh, Robert," she said, her voice shaky. "I'm just . . . overwhelmed, to put it mildly." Her voice dropped to a whisper. "I don't think any man has ever loved me before."

His heart melted. She looked so shy and vulnerable, sitting there in the moonlight, no longer independent and cocky. At least she didn't look scared. Not yet. He lifted her hands and kissed them.

"You've never let a man love you," he said. "Or rather, you've protected yourself by dating men who wouldn't love you, who would only chase after the magic."

"But am I so different from them?"

"You're the one who said we didn't have to fly around the stars to get to never-never land. Magic's where you make it. I can feel it here between us. If you try, I know you could, too."

She looked down at him, her brows drawn together in the way they did when she was puzzled or uncertain. "Magic. Love," she murmured, as if to herself. "I suppose they could be the same." She smiled winsomely. "Does that make you Peter Pan?"

He laughed and stood up, pulling her into his arms. "I'd prefer Merlin. I rather like the Camelot analogy."

"My cat will get confused if I start calling you Merlin." She gently bit his earlobe.

"Well, then," he said, fiddling with one of the straps of her gown, "you can call me wonderful—" the strap came untied, and the gown fell away to reveal one breast "—magnificent—" he fondled her breast with one hand while he loosened the remaining tie with the other "—fabulous—" her head fell to his chest as his fingers plucked at her already taut nipples "—incredible—" with a swivel of her hips, the gown fell to the floor "—fantastic—" he lowered his mouth to her breast as she hastily unfastened and unzipped his jeans "—stupendous—" with one quick movement they both rid him of his pants "—marv— Ah, love," he cried as she caressed his throbbing manhood. He carried her to the bed while he could still walk.

THE NEARER THEY DREW to New York, the greater Robert's anxiety became. Despite the wonderful week and a half he and Aubrey had spent together, despite the closeness he felt was between them, he was worried. There was no denying that Aubrey was an independent woman with very strong ideas about how she wanted to live her life. Although she was willing to give their relationship a chance, willing to fight her fear of commitment and dependence, he knew their relationship wasn't going to be smooth sailing.

He leaned his head back and closed his eyes. His body swayed slightly as Aubrey pulled into the left lane to pass another car. She had insisted on sharing the drive with him and was now covering the last leg to New York. They were on the Connecticut Turnpike, which was crowded with cars, the slowest of which Robert figured was going sixty miles an hour. He wasn't at all surprised that Aubrey spent most of her time in the far left lane, her hands relaxed and confident on the wheel as she sang along with the radio. He didn't bother to lean over and check the speedometer to see how fast she was going. He really didn't want to know. She was a good driver, though, and he trusted her capabilities. The other drivers, however...

Still, they made it in one piece, and when Aubrey turned onto Robert's street, she cheerfully said it had been a fun drive and she'd only seen her life pass before her eyes three times. Robert smiled and thought about how much he loved this woman. Dauntless in so many ways, yet vulnerable in the most surprising and endearing ways. Would she come to love him?

He directed her to his apartment building, and she double-parked in front of the brownstone. As he opened his door he saw her gazing avidly at the building, as if she could see into his apartment. Casually he asked, "Would you like to come up?"

"No." She shook her head. "I'd have to find a place to park the car, and I'm awfully tired."

He interpreted her answer as, "It's too soon," and nodded. They got out of the car, and he pulled his bags from the trunk.

"Well," she said, after slamming the trunk lid down, "thank you."

He set his bags down and pulled her into his arms. "My pleasure." He kissed her deeply, thoroughly, painfully reluctant to let her go. "Call me when you get home, so I'll know you got there safely."

She opened her mouth, to protest, he was sure, then shut it and nodded. "I...uh..." She shoved her hands into her pockets. "I guess I'll see you around."

He smiled, enjoying her nervousness. At least he had some effect on her. "You can count on it. I'll call you tomorrow."

"I told you—"

"I know," he interrupted her. "You don't like me to say that. Well, you're going to have to get used to it, because I mean it and intend to keep on saying it. Maybe after I follow through a couple hundred times, you'll believe me."

"Believe—you—"

He stopped her sputtering with a quick kiss, then picked up his bags and walked away. When he reached his front door and looked back, he saw that she was still standing in the street, still looking bemused. He waved and yelled, "Don't forget to call me when you get home."

She didn't respond for a moment, then suddenly laughed. "All right!" she shouted before getting back in her car.

He watched her drive away, then unlocked the door and stepped inside the brownstone. a relieved and happy smile on his face.

ROBERT DASHED up the stairs of his apartment building, swearing under his breath. He was due at Aubrey's in ten minutes; obviously he was going to be late. He unlocked his apartment door, rushed inside and dropped his briefcase on the floor as he headed for the phone. This relationship was going to give him an ulcer, he thought as he punched out Aubrey's number. In the two weeks since they'd been back from Maine, they'd seen hardly anything of each other. He had dropped into Alex's several times, but only being able to see Aubrey with a bar between them and to talk to her briefly had been frustrating. Once she had come downtown to join him for lunch, but the hurried, public meeting hadn't been satisfying. It wouldn't be so bad, he thought as he listened to Aubrey's phone ring, if she didn't insist on using much of her free time to see other friends. He understood but still resented his apparent low priority on her scale. Just this past Tuesday night, for instance, when he—

"Hello?" Aubrey said into the phone.

"Hi, Aubrey," he said. He nestled the phone against his shoulder and began loosening his tie. "I'm afraid I'm going to be a little late."

"Where are you?"

"Home."

"Yes, I'd say you're going to be a little late. Well, all right. I'll expect you when I see you."

"Aubrey, I'm sorry. I...I'll explain when I get there."

"Okay. See you in a bit. Bye."

"Bye." He hung up the phone. "Damn!" She was obviously disappointed that he was late, but she'd also sounded hurt. Cripes, he thought, stalking into his bedroom, at least he'd been nice enough to call.

By the time Robert had changed into lightweight slacks and a polo shirt, his mood had improved to a minor degree. It had been a bad day, a bad week, actually, and his worrying that things weren't working out with Aubrey wasn't helping. At least they had tonight, just the two of them, and they were spending all of Sunday together. That wasn't so bad, he told himself, and his step was a little lighter as he left his apartment.

Ten minutes later Robert arrived at Aubrey's mammoth apartment building. He had been lucky to get a cab practically right in front of his apartment, but had questioned his luck when the driver had floored it, trying to beat the yellow light more than half a block down the narrow street. Still, at least he'd gotten to Aubrey's quickly.

The doorman buzzed him in and called up to Aubrey's apartment as Robert waited for the elevator. When he got off on the eleventh floor, she was standing at her open door, waiting for him.

"Hurry!" she called as he started down the hall toward her.

Puzzled, he quickened his pace. She gave him a brief kiss when he reached her, then dragged him into the apartment. "Five minutes isn't a very long time," she said as she led him down the hall to the kitchen.

Indeed, when they reached the kitchen, Robert saw that there was only a minute left on the ticking timer. "What are you making?" he asked.

"It's a surprise." She grabbed two pot holders and stood in front of the oven, staring at the timer.

Robert smiled, amused by her intensity. Her earlier disappointment and hurt were apparently gone, and he wondered if her reaction had had anything to do with what was in the oven. If she'd been counting on him to arrive promptly, as he usually did, and had planned this surprise accordingly, his being late must have thrown her.

The timer pinged. "Aha!" she cried, and flung open the oven door. She reached inside and pulled out the most amazing confection. Robert stared at it as she carefully set it on a plate.

She glanced at him. "Never had this before, huh? You're in for a treat. Here, you carry these." She handed him two glass plates, two forks, a large knife and a pie server. "And I'll take this." She picked up the plate and started down the hall to her bedroom. Robert obediently followed her.

When he entered the room, he lifted his brows in surprise. The room was dim, illuminated only by a small lamp near the door and a pair of candles on the table by the French doors. The door to her living room was open, and through it he could hear Rimsky-Korsakov's *Scheherazade*. The whole effect was unabashedly romantic, and he loved it.

"Come sit," Aubrey instructed as she set the dessert down on the table.

He put down the dishes he was carrying and sat. "Are you going to tell me what it is?" he asked as she slowly sank the knife into the center of her masterpiece.

"Baked Alaska."

"Ah." He had been right about the careful timing. All that ice cream would melt very quickly if it couldn't be served immediately. He put a forkful in his mouth and sighed with contentment and approval. "Delicious," he said.

"Thank you," she said, then disappeared briefly to get their coffee from the kitchen. "I hope I didn't sound too annoyed over the phone, but the one time you decide to be late . . ."

He laughed and picked up her hand and kissed it. "I'm sorry. Maybe I'd better stop telling you I'll call now, too." She shook her head. "I'm growing on you, huh?" She nodded, grinning impishly around her coffee cup. "Well, would you like to hear why I was late?"

"Do tell."

Actually, he ended up telling her about his entire week, the case he was working feverishly on, his attempt to placate the irritable and volatile client, the late nights and early mornings and no lunches. And how the client had dropped in unexpectedly that evening, at quarter to five, and hadn't left until after seven.

"Poor Robert," she said, stroking his cheek. "Why didn't you tell me any of this earlier on the phone or when you dropped by Alex's?"

He shrugged and ate some more baked Alaska.

"Robert Browning," she said sternly, "you've been holding out on me! And you call *me* evasive."

He looked up at her. "I really didn't think you'd be interested in what a stuffy lawyer did during the day." He was smiling slightly, but Aubrey detected defensiveness in his voice.

"That may be true," she said softly. "I don't particularly care about stuffy lawyers, but I do care about you. Of course I want to know about your job, what happens to you during the day, whether you're happy or not. Do you think I always ask you how your day went just to be polite? You should know me better than that, Robert."

He stared at her, bemused. Until now, he hadn't realized how much of his life he didn't share with her. On some subconscious level he must have been worried that she wouldn't be interested, would grow bored, and he would lose her. What kind of relationship was that? He wanted to know intimately all aspects of her life, yet he was afraid to share his own.

He reached across the table and took one of her hands. "I'm sorry. I didn't realize how much I wasn't telling you. I'll do better from now on."

"I hope so," she whispered, staring into his eyes. "It hasn't bothered me that much, but occasionally I've wondered if you think I'm not bright enough to understand all your legalese—" he squeezed her hand and started to protest, but she rushed on "—or if you're embarrassed to introduce me to your friends because I'm a trifle . . . odd."

He squeezed her hand again, then stood up, urging her to do the same. "Odd?" he repeated. "That is not the word I'd use to describe you." Indeed not, he thought, his gaze sweeping over her. Words like *wonderful* and *beautiful* and *classy* came to mind instead. She was wearing an oversize white blouse, the sleeves partly rolled up and the tail hanging out. The shirt was anchored at her hips by a wide leather belt. Her legs were encased in tight, straight-leg black jeans, and at her throat was a lace scarf, wound around her neck once and tied in a loose knot.

"No," he murmured, drawing her into his arms, "you are not odd." He lowered his head to hers and brushed fleeting kisses across her lips as he spoke. "You might be distinctive, unique, one in a million, but never—"

She held his head still with her hands and pressed her mouth firmly to his, effectively silencing him. He moaned and pulled her body against his. So long, he thought as he parted her lips with his tongue. So long— a week—since he'd held her in his arms and kissed her the way he wanted to. He weaved the fingers of one hand through her hair, holding her head still as he assaulted her mouth. She made tantalizing little sounds of excitement and brushed her hips back and forth across his. Robert was thinking that he couldn't wait to get their clothes off before he made love to her, when she started pulling away from him. He hauled her back against him, his mouth seeking hers, but she pressed her fingers to his lips, stopping him.

"The downstairs buzzer just rang," she said, her voice a little unsteady. "Someone's coming up."

He cupped one of her breasts in one hand and ran his thumb over the nipple, watching with satisfaction as her eyes darkened and glazed over slightly. "Let someone else let them in," he whispered.

"Can't," she said, shaking her head weakly. "No one else is home."

"Then let's pretend we're not home."

Even as he suggested it, he knew she wouldn't go for it. She crossed the room to the dresser and brushed her hair, then adjusted her shirt. She had just turned to speak to him when they heard a knock on the door.

She shrugged helplessly. "Maybe it's the Fuller Brush man and I can get rid of him quickly."

Robert smiled, then sat down and picked up his coffee cup. Aubrey walked to the front door, wondering who would be dropping in at nine o'clock on a Friday night. The Sullivans were out of town, and Maggie was heaven knows where. She opened the door, and her eyes widened with surprise. Standing before her were two close friends, Patti Black and George Hopper. Patti looked tearful, George defensive. *Uh-oh*, Aubrey thought. *There goes the quiet evening alone with Robert.*

"Patti! George!" she exclaimed, trying to smile. "What a surprise. Come on in."

"Sorry to barge in, P.T.," George said, "but Patti insisted."

"It was your idea," Patti contradicted him, and swept into the apartment.

"Uh, just go into my living room," Aubrey said, closing the door after George. "I'll be with you in a sec."

She dashed into her bedroom and closed the connecting door. She turned to face Robert, and found him looking at her with an expression that was partially amused, partially resigned.

"Not the Fuller Brush man, I guess," he said.

"No. Would you like to come meet two of my friends?"

He sighed. "I'd much prefer staying in here with you, but I suppose there's no helping it."

She smiled at him. "I am sorry, Robert. I'll make it up to you."

"Either that," he said, standing and walking over to her, "or I'll have my revenge." He kissed her quickly. "Shall we?"

Patti and George had made themselves comfortable at opposite ends of the living room, she in one corner of the couch, he in an antique morris chair. Aubrey took one look at the stormy expressions on their faces and groaned inwardly. It was going to be a long night.

"Patti, George, I'd like you to meet a friend of mine. This is Robert Browning. Robert, this is Patti Black and George Hopper." Robert and George shook hands. "Patti is a singer, mostly jazz and blues, and George is an archaeologist. Robert is a—"

"'And so fall asleep, Love,/Loved by thee,'" Patti interrupted.

Another person who could quote Browning, Robert thought with respect, and nodded to her.

"Are you a poet?" George asked him.

"No, a lawyer."

"Hmph," Patti said. "Well, at least we don't need a lawyer this time around." She glared at George.

"How about some tea?" Aubrey suggested, fore-stalling whatever remark George had been about to make. "Could you help me, Patti?"

The singer rose from the couch and followed Aubrey down the hall to the kitchen.

"Just have a seat," Aubrey said as she filled the tea-kettle. She set it on a burner, then sat down across the table from Patti. "Now tell me what's wrong."

Patti promptly burst into tears and fumbled in the pocket of her electric-blue trousers for a clean tissue. "George wants to get married," she said between sniffles and sobs.

Aubrey looked at her with bewilderment. "But that's great, isn't it? Unless it's not you he wants to marry."

Patti blotted her eyes, then blew her nose. "Oh, it's me he wants to marry. And as soon as possible. He's going to Africa in a few months."

"Africa!" Aubrey's eyes brightened with interest. "How fabulous. You'll go with him, of course."

Patti stared blankly at her. "Go with him! And do what? Sing to the crocodiles?"

"Oh. Right." Aubrey got up and began preparing the tea. She rinsed the teapot with hot water and threw into it a few teaspoons of the caffeine-free herbal tea she knew her friends liked. She found four clean mugs and set them on a tray, along with a bowl of honey. Obviously, she thought as she stared out the kitchen window, Patti and George had come here for her advice, wanting her to act as mediator. And why not? She was the one who had introduced them, who had convinced them to go out on a second date when they'd each re-ported separately that the first date had been horrendous, the one who had thought their moving in together was a splendid idea. What could she tell them this time, though? She could empathize with George's wanting to go on a dig to Africa, and with Patti's not wanting to give up a good career, and with both of them not wanting to lose each other. Relationships certainly could be a problem.

The teakettle whistled, and she filled the pot. Patti carried the tray back to the living room; Aubrey followed with the teapot. She wasn't surprised to see the two men in lively conversation, scarcely noticing when the women entered the room.

"Ahem," Aubrey said, clearing her throat loudly. Robert and George looked up, faintly puzzled by the interruption. "Tea, gentlemen?"

"Sure," George said. "Sorry we didn't help. Fascinating discussion, though."

"Oh?" Aubrey filled a mug and handed it to Patti. "What about?"

"Women who are afraid of commitment."

Aubrey's eyes widened, and she stared at Robert. What had he been saying to her friend?

"I am not afraid of commitment!" Patti said.

Aubrey handed a mug to George.

"Then marry me!" he said.

"Just so that I can wave goodbye as you board the plane to Africa?" Patti retorted.

Aubrey handed a mug to Robert.

"I told you you can come with me."

Aubrey filled a mug for herself.

"And what would I do there? What about my career?"

"Does anybody want honey?" Aubrey asked.

Patti and George were again glaring at each other and didn't answer. Aubrey looked at Robert.

"I think we all need a little honey," he said.

Aubrey laughed. "You're probably right. How about it, Patti? George? Want to lighten up a little?"

Neither Patti nor George spoke for a minute; then George leaned back in his chair and sighed.

"You're right, Aubrey," he said. "Sorry about the crack about commitment, Patti. I didn't mean it."

"Yes, you did," Patti said miserably. "But you're wrong. I'm not afraid of commitment. I'm afraid of leaving everything I know to go traipsing off to Africa, totally dependent on you."

"She's got a point there," Aubrey said. "Total dependency is a scary thing."

"No one ever has to be totally dependent," Robert said. "Not if they don't want to be. Just keep a return-trip ticket in your back pocket, Patti."

"It's not that simple," Aubrey said, surprising herself with the heat of her words. "It's more than a matter of going and coming back. It's the emotional impact of giving up so much on the hope that one person won't abandon you."

She stopped speaking abruptly, startled by what she had said. It was the first time she had revealed her fear so blatantly. She looked up to find Robert gazing intently at her.

"I know it's not that easy to trust someone," he said softly, "to depend on him or her so much. I didn't mean to belittle the courage it takes to make that kind of commitment, the emotional impact it would have."

"But where does one find that trust?" she whispered.

Patti looked from Aubrey, to Robert, to George. "Good point, Aubrey," she said. "And I think that's what George and I need to do right now, find that trust." She stood up. "And we really should find it on our own and not interrupt your evening."

"Oh, no," Aubrey protested. "If you feel you need to talk some more, stay. And George, I want to hear more about what you're going to be doing in Africa." She paused. "I've always wanted to go to Africa."

George laughed. "You've always wanted to be an archaeologist, too. That's how we met," he added, turning to Robert. "A couple of years ago, we were on the same subway. I was reading a text on archaeology, and the woman beside me was reading over my shoulder. I looked up, and she immediately started talking to me about archaeology, asking if I was an archaeologist, what digs I'd worked on. For a layperson she sure knew a great deal about it."

Aubrey shrugged and looked at the ceiling. "I read a lot."

"She also knew a great deal about jazz," Patti added.

"And I listen to records a lot."

"And she knows almost nothing about law," Robert said.

She cocked her head coyly at him. "Give me time."

They all laughed, and none of them realized the front door had opened and closed until they heard Maggie call, "P.T.! Guess what?"

"In the living room!" Aubrey called back.

Maggie burst through the door, her eyes bright, a wide smile on her face. "P.T., I—" She paused. "Hello,

Robert, Patti, George. Oh, I'm so glad you're here. You can help me celebrate. I just came back from dinner with that guy from the magazine in San Francisco. I got the job!"

"Maggie!" Aubrey jumped up from the couch and gave her friend a big hug. "Oh, congratulations! That's fabulous. When do you go?"

"In two weeks."

"We have to have a party," Patti said instantly. "Downtown. Maybe at the Blue Note. Or even one of the newer clubs in SoHo."

"We can have it in the East River for all I care," Maggie said. "I'm so excited."

"Congratulations, Maggie," George said, kissing her on the cheek. "Splendid, really." He glanced at Patti. "Good thing you're not seeing anyone now."

"Who's to see in New York?" Maggie said. "Present company excepted, of course."

"Considering San Francisco's male population," Robert said, "I can't imagine you're going to have better luck out there."

Maggie sighed. "But if you're in San Francisco, who cares?"

Aubrey laughed. "Sit down and have some tea, Maggie. I'll go get what's left of a very sloppy baked Alaska, and we can finish it off."

When she returned to the living room with the melting dessert and plates and forks, she found everyone involved in a discussion on the merits and drawbacks of life in San Francisco. Everyone had been there except her, she thought with some disappointment. Merlin, she saw, had appeared and settled on Robert's lap. *Nice when the two males in your life get along.*

After the baked Alaska had been served and everyone was happily eating, Robert turned to Aubrey.

"Would you answer one question for me?"

She shrugged and said, "Sure."

"Since I met you, people have been calling you P.T. I've been trying for a month to figure out what it means. Would you please tell me?"

George, Patti and Maggie burst into laughter, and Aubrey felt herself start to blush.

"Yes, well . . . um," she mumbled, "it means . . ."

"If you don't tell him, I will," Maggie said.

"Popsicle toes," Aubrey said quickly.

"Popsicle toes?" Robert repeated, obviously confused.

"You mean, you've never noticed her toes?" Maggie asked him. "Even on vacation?"

Robert looked even more befuddled. "What about her toes?"

"I wasn't wearing any on vacation," Aubrey interrupted. "You—" she looked directly at Maggie "—forgot to pack any."

"Pack *toes*?" Robert said.

"No, polish," Aubrey explained. "Of course I've got toes. I just . . . polish them."

"With what?" he asked. "Lemon-flavored Pledge?"

She laughed. "No, no. Fingernail polish. Or rather, toenail polish." She sighed. "I guess it all started back when I was thirteen or so, when I wanted to polish my fingernails and my mother wouldn't let me. So I polished my toenails instead. It was fun. I could use all those wild, zany colors. It got so that my feet looked . . . well, naked without any polish. I can't remember who started the nickname here in New York, but it's hung around for five or six years."

"P.T.," Robert said musingly. "I kind of like it."

Aubrey groaned. "Of course. I think I'm the only one who doesn't."

"Well," George said, standing up, "I think Patti and I should be going now."

"Yes, we should," Patti said, also standing. "Thanks so much, Aubrey."

"Why don't you give me a call tomorrow?" Aubrey said, kissing Patti on the cheek. "We should get together for lunch."

"All right," Patti said.

Goodbyes were said all around before Aubrey escorted George and Patti to the door. "You'll work it out," she said as she hugged each of them.

The living room was empty of people and dirty dishes when she returned to it. She walked down the hall to the kitchen and found Robert and Maggie side by side at the sink, he washing, she drying.

"An unknown talent," Aubrey said. "Robert, why didn't you tell me you were so handy in the kitchen?"

He grinned at her. "I was waiting to impress you with my real stellar qualities if all else failed."

"Hmm," Maggie said, her gaze running up and down Robert's lean body. "It doesn't look to me like anything on you would *ever* fail."

"Maggie!" Aubrey exclaimed as Robert laughed. "He's *my* guest."

"Oh! Right you are." Maggie dropped the dish towel and headed out of the kitchen. "So you play in the soapsuds with him."

Aubrey shook her head and picked up the dish towel. She was just reaching for a plate when Robert's long arms caught her.

"Alone at last," he said.

"Alone and *wet*," she retorted. "If you get my shirt wet . . ."

"You'll have to take it off." He kissed her. "That's the idea, love."

"Lovely idea, but not in the kitchen, okay?"

He sighed in mock despair and dropped his arms. "Okay. Besides," he added, "we need to talk."

She shot him a quick glance. "Let's finish the dishes first."

After they were through in the kitchen, they returned to her living room. Aubrey put a Joan Baez album on the turntable, then sat down beside Robert on the couch.

"Yes?" she asked. "What did you want to talk about?"

He picked up her hand and studied it, turning it over to trace the lines on the palm, then placed it on his thigh. "Your romantic evening got kind of shot to hell," he said finally.

"Kind of. I'm sorry about Patti and George, but I guess my friends just consider me available at all times."

He nodded. "They have a rather serious problem they need to work out."

She sighed. "I hope they don't break up. They're wonderful together."

"So are we."

The somberness in Robert's voice forced her to look at him. "I know, Robert."

"What's holding you back, Aubrey? I know you're an independent woman, I know you have dozens of people vying for your time. Still, I don't know why I'm such a low priority with you." His voice rose slightly. "I'm your lover, damn it, and I only get to see you once a week!"

She pulled her hand from his and turned to face him. "Don't put all the blame on me. You're the one who cancelled our lunch date this week."

"But who cancelled our dinner date Tuesday night?" he shot back, then immediately relented. "I don't want to fight with you, Aubrey," he said softly, smoothing her hair back with one hand. "I do want to understand, though. What are you afraid of?"

"I'm afraid I'm going to leave you," she said, staring at her hands.

"Why?" he asked. "Aside from the normal reasons why a relationship ends, why do you think you'll leave me?"

"Oh, I don't know, Robert." Her voice was high and strained. "I've never stayed before. I've never done *this* before." She drew in a deep, shaking breath. "I'm just afraid."

"Aubrey." He gently pulled her into his arms and nestled her head against his shoulder. "I'm afraid, too. But I love you, and I know this is going to work." He kissed her forehead. "You can depend on Sir Lancelot."

"My knight in shining armor," she murmured.

"That's right." He tilted her chin up so that she was looking at him. "Do you trust me? Do you at least trust me not to leave you?"

She didn't answer. She just held on to him, her arms growing tighter and tighter around him. Finally he heard her muffled voice. "I trust you."

I THINK THIS WAS A BAD IDEA, Robert," Aubrey said. "Tell the cab driver to take me back to my apartment."

Robert smiled and slipped his arm around her shoulders. "Nonsense, sweetheart. You're going to have a great time."

"Huh," she said disbelievingly, nervously fiddling with her necklace.

They were on their way to a party, a celebration for a member of the firm Robert worked for; the man had just been made a partner. Robert had told her there would probably only be about fifty people there, and that although most of them were lawyers, they were all very nice people. His father wouldn't be there, and Aubrey was thankful for that small favor. Robert had asked her to come to the party a week ago, and she had spent the past seven days alternating between supreme confidence and extraordinary agitation.

She didn't have a thing to wear, she'd moaned to Maggie, and wouldn't know how to act. She'd feel like a child at a grown-ups' party and was certain that everyone would instantly tag her as an unsophisticated upstart from the southwest.

"You're the one," Maggie had said sternly, "who wanted to be part of his life. Here's your chance."

"I'd much rather just meet him for lunch."

Actually, she'd done that this past week. He had set aside two hours on Tuesday, and they'd eaten at South Street Seaport, then wandered around the area, ducking into interesting shops and admiring the renovated buildings. Robert had also brought two friends to Alex's on Wednesday night. They were the first friends of his she'd met, and she had been thrilled at this further indication that Robert was opening his life to her.

But a party on Park Avenue! Wasn't this a bit much all at once? She had asked herself that time and time again. What would a bartender have in common with a bunch of overeducated lawyers?

"Would you relax?" Robert said to her as the cab stopped in front of an elegant East Side apartment building.

She peered out her window at the soaring building and the uniformed doorman who was walking toward their cab. "Isn't this where Jackie Onassis lives?" she muttered.

Robert chuckled as he pocketed the change the cab driver gave him. "No," he said. "She's over on Fifth Avenue, not Park."

The doorman opened Aubrey's door and extended a hand. With all the panache she could manage, she lightly grasped the white-gloved hand and stepped from the cab.

"Thank you," she murmured.

"My pleasure, ma'am," he said, touching the brim of his cap. "Good evening, sir," he added when Robert joined them.

"Good evening. We're here for the Benton party," Robert said.

"Of course," the doorman said, and led them into the building.

They rode up alone in the elevator to the twelfth floor. Aubrey couldn't keep her hands still. She smoothed her hair back, bloused her bright blue shirt over the waistband of her cream-colored silk pants, checked her high-heeled blue sandals to make sure there wasn't anything clinging to them. Robert grasped her hand.

"You look fine," he said, raising her hand to his lips for a kiss. His gaze swept over her, from her French-braided hair to her toenails, painted a plum color. "More than fine. Fabulous." He quickly kissed her on the lips, careful not to smear her lipstick, then smiled down at her. "They're just people, Aubrey. You're good with people."

She nodded as the elevator doors opened, then took a deep breath and stepped out into the hallway. Nice carpet, she thought, thinking of the tile that covered the halls of her own building. Robert took her arm and led her a short way down the hall to a door. He knocked, and the door was opened instantly by a woman.

"Robert!" she exclaimed. "We didn't think you were going to make it."

"Sorry we're late." He exchanged kisses on the cheek with the woman. "Traffic was horrendous."

That was a blatant lie, Aubrey thought as Robert drew her into the apartment behind him. *She* had been late, her nerves having got the better of her, making it impossible for her to decide what to wear. She appreciated Robert's gallantry.

"This is Aubrey Jones," he was saying. "Aubrey, this is Alice Benton, Harry Benton's wife."

"Hello," Aubrey said, shaking the woman's hand and smiling. Alice Benton was a very attractive woman, perhaps in her late forties. Her short hair was sleek and chic, and her simply styled designer dress was of the latest fashion. Aubrey had the sudden urge to announce that she had bought her silk pants in a second-hand clothing store.

"Hello, Aubrey," Alice said warmly. "So glad you could come. Are you a lawyer?"

"No, I'm not."

"Oh, I'm so glad. Sometimes I think everyone in the world must be a lawyer." She tucked Aubrey's arm under her own. "So you probably won't know many people here. Robert," she said over her shoulder as she started leading Aubrey away, "why don't you get yourself and Aubrey a drink, and I'll start introducing her around."

Aubrey glanced back, saw Robert give her an encouraging smile, then turned to speak to the first person Alice Benton was introducing to her. Within ten minutes Aubrey decided Robert had been right. She had had nothing to worry about. These were just people, and she was good with people. At the moment she was sitting on a sofa in the living room, a man on either side of her. Fascinated to hear she was a bartender, they had sat her down and demanded a detailed description of what her job was like. Aubrey was happily obliging them.

Across the room, Robert was talking with Harry Benton, the new partner.

"Nice-looking woman, Robert," Harry said, nodding toward Aubrey.

"Tom and Mike seem to think so, too," Robert said, referring to the men sitting with her. One was practically leaning over her, his arm across the back of the sofa behind her. The other man's leg looked very, very close to hers.

Harry glanced at Robert and grinned. "Think you need to go over there and make it clear to those fellows who came with whom?"

For a moment Robert considered doing just that, but he chuckled. "Are you kidding? Aubrey would kill me." She looked up at that moment and saw him, and he waved. "She wouldn't appreciate my caveman tactics," he continued to Harry. "She's a very independent woman."

Oh, damn you, Robert, Aubrey thought. *Quit talking to Harry and get over here.* The two men were now actively vying for her attention. One of them—she wasn't sure if his name was Tom or Mike—was leaning uncomfortably close to her and kept patting her knee as he spoke.

"I need to get a fresh drink," the other man said. He stood up abruptly and disappeared, leaving Aubrey alone with her unwanted suitor. At least she had room to maneuver, she thought as she slid a few inches away from the man.

"I really should go and find Robert," she said, and started to get up.

Tom—Mike?—put his hand on her arm to detain her. "Is that who you came with, Robert Browning? What's a carefree girl like you doing with an old stick-in-the-mud like Robert?"

She almost laughed, remembering how un-stick-in-the-mudlike Robert had been when they'd danced in the rain on York Beach. She removed her arm from the other man's grasp. "Yes, I came with Robert," she said, "and my relationship with him is none of your business." She again tried to get up, but his arm dropped from the back of the sofa to her shoulders, and he leaned even closer.

"Don't get mad at me," he said. "I was just teasin'. Hey, I think Robert's a great guy. He just doesn't seem like your type."

"You think you're more Aubrey's type, Tom?" Robert asked.

Both Aubrey and Tom looked up to find Robert standing over them, a drink in each hand, an amused expression on his face.

"Hey there, Robert." Tom leaped to his feet. "I was just keepin' Aubrey here company until you got back."

"I'm back now."

"Right. So I'll go."

"Right."

Tom hurried away, and Robert sat down beside Aubrey. "Here," he said, handing her a glass. "I got you a melon ball."

"Thank you."

"Was he bothering you?"

"No." She shook her head and laughed. "At least he certainly proved that my fears about this evening were groundless. You lawyers really are just ordinary folk."

He raised a brow. "Ordinary? Me?"

"Oh, no." She pushed his hair back from his forehead, watching with delight as it fell into place. "You are definitely not ordinary." She leaned closer. "Ordinary people don't go to never-never land."

Robert felt a familiar tightening in his loins as he caught a whiff of her perfume. When he'd sat on her bed earlier, watching her dress, he had almost suggested that they not go to this party. With her so close to him now, her hand resting lightly on his thigh, her dark eyes filled with humor and desire, he was having difficulty remembering exactly where they were. What power she had over him, he thought, covering her hand with his and squeezing it lightly.

He might as well have caressed her breast, Aubrey thought, as her whole body seemed to melt at Robert's casual touch. The effect this man had on her was . . . magical. Oh, yes, she thought, he was magic. The last of her doubts and fears ebbed away, replaced by a blissful serenity.

She turned her hand up so that she was holding his and whispered, "I love you, Robert."

He blinked in astonishment. "What?"

"I love you. Would you like me to say it louder?"

"No!" He briefly pressed his fingers against her lips. "Oh, Aubrey. What possessed you to say that now?"

She smiled happily. "I just realized it, and it seemed to me you'd been waiting long enough to hear me say it."

"Aubrey." He caressed her cheek, then smoothed back a few stray tendrils of hair that had come free. "I would have willingly waited a lot longer."

Alice Benton suddenly slid onto the coffee table and gazed intently at both of them. "You know, if you two would like to leave now, it's okay with me. I promise I won't think you're ducking out early because it's a lousy party."

Robert was nonplussed, but Aubrey just smiled. "Thank you, Alice. And it's not a lousy party at all. It's a wonderful one."

Alice stood and winked. "Love'll do that to you."

Robert watched Alice walk away, still uncertain how she could have known what he and Aubrey had been saying, then turned to Aubrey. "Would you like to go now?"

She nodded eagerly. "That is, if you'd like to."

He smiled. "Are you kidding?"

Despite their desire to leave quickly, it was another twenty minutes until they could make it to the door. They had to locate both the host and hostess, and in the meantime got drawn into half a dozen conversations.

"You were a hit," Robert said to her as they waited for the elevator.

"I was?"

"Quite a few people mentioned to me that they thought you were fascinating and where had I been hiding you."

She laughed. "Did you tell them you'd kidnapped me and carried me off to the coast of Maine?"

"And ruin my reputation as a stick-in-the-mud?"

They were both laughing when the elevator arrived and they stepped into it. The instant the doors closed, trapping them alone in the small space, their laughter stopped. Without pause they turned to each other, lips meeting, arms enfolding. The kiss was gentle, tender, as if they both felt the need to treat with care Aubrey's young love. When they drew apart, their eyes met.

"I love you," he said.

"I love you," she said.

Robert's apartment was only about ten blocks away, and since the night was warm and clear, they decided to walk there. They didn't speak as they strolled along, arm in arm. Aubrey divided her attention between the man at her side and the charming brownstones and town houses they were walking past. In her euphoric state, she magnanimously decided the East Side wasn't so bad, after all.

Robert's apartment was on the third floor of a small brownstone. The front door opened into a hallway that connected the living room in the front to the bedroom in the back. The living room wasn't large, but the egg-shell-white walls gave the impression of spaciousness. Light-colored drapes framed the two windows that overlooked the quiet street; a steel-blue carpet covered the floor. The furniture was solid but comfortable-looking, and Aubrey was entranced by an old sea captain's chest that stood between the windows.

"This is great, Robert," she said. "How long have you been here?"

"About four years."

"What are these?" she said suddenly, picking up three books from the coffee table. "White's *The Once and Future King* and *The Book of Merlyn*—and Malory's *Morte D'Arthur*?" She grinned at Robert.

"They're good books," he said defensively, taking them from her and setting them back down on the table.

"I'm crushed, Robert," she said, teasing. "Here I thought all your chivalry came to you naturally, but you've actually been studying it in books."

He gave her a threatening look. "Would you like to see the rest of the apartment?"

She smothered a giggle. "Of course."

He led her into the kitchen, beyond a small dining alcove. It was quite small and startlingly neat and clean.

"Don't do much cooking, do you?" she said, peering into the refrigerator. Inside was wine, beer, orange juice, cheese, bread, eggs and not much else.

"If you're really hungry, Aubrey..."

"Oh, no." She shut the door and smiled brightly at him. "Just looking." Just nervous, she added silently. She loved Robert, believed and trusted him when he said he loved her. Still, she was unnerved being in his home, on his territory, as it were.

"The rest of the apartment's back here," he said, leading her down the hall to the back of the building. A good-sized bathroom was to the right, his bedroom to the left. The bedroom wasn't very large, which was why, Aubrey figured, the bed seemed predominant. It was made of dark wood and matched the dresser opposite it. On the far side of the room was a window, and she looked out. Three stories down was a courtyard with a small garden.

"It really is a wonderful apartment," she said, turning back to Robert. "You must love it."

He smiled lazily at her and began walking toward her. "Oh, I do," he said. "I love it almost as much as I love you." He had reached her and slid his arms around her waist. His warm mouth explored the length of her slender neck. "Almost as much as I love making love to you."

The feel of his hard body against hers sparked such longing within Aubrey that she had to clutch his shoulders to keep from falling. Her nipples tightened almost painfully, and her body seemed to be on fire. She feverishly sought his mouth with hers, and they clung to each other as their kiss exploded in rising passion. His hands slid down to her hips, and he pressed her against him, showing her his eagerness to share their love completely.

"Robert," she gasped as he released her mouth and began tracing her ear with his tongue, "I think we'd better sit down before we fall down."

"Hmm," he said, and backed to the bed, not loosening his hold on her. He sat on the edge of the bed, then lay back, pulling her with him. She settled her body on top of his, melting into him.

"It was a long week without you," she murmured, kissing his throat.

"We had lunch together, and I dropped by Alex's." His hands had freed her shirttail and were now smoothing over the bare skin of her back.

"Yes, but we haven't done *this* all week."

"Aha." He lifted his head and looked her in the eye. "You just admitted you only want me for my body."

She grinned, and her hand slid between their bodies to toy with his belt buckle. "There's a time and place for everything."

He grabbed her wrist, halting her teasing, and rolled over so that she was beneath him. "I agree. And every night in my bed is the time and place for us."

She froze. What, she thought, momentarily unable to speak.

He smiled tenderly at her shocked expression. "Didn't mean to startle you, love," he said, "but I mean it. I want you with me every night."

He wanted to marry her? She was still numb with surprise. She remembered a phone call a few days earlier from Patti and George, who had announced that they had worked out their problems and would be marrying in six weeks. They had both been ecstatic, and Aubrey had been happy for them. It had also started her wondering if she and Robert . . .

She blinked. "Every night, Robert?" she repeated. "What do you mean?"

Dare he say the word *marry*, he wondered. Dare he get down on one knee and, like a knight of old, proclaim his undying love and beg her to be his wife? No. He didn't dare. He was too afraid of asking for too much and thereby losing her.

"I mean," he said quietly, "that I want to live with you, to be with you all the time."

He wanted to live with her. Aubrey sat up, mindlessly tucking her blouse back in and smoothing her pants. He didn't want to marry her, just live with her. Well, wouldn't that be better, less constricting? She could always leave without the hassle of a divorce. But no, she realized, that wasn't what she wanted. She wanted to be completely committed to Robert or not at all.

"I love you, Aubrey," he went on. "And you love me. We should be—we *need* to be together." He slid off the bed and began pacing the floor, his anxiety at her lack of response needing release. "Maybe I'm putting this badly. Remember how wonderful that week in Maine was, and how frustrating it's been here in New York, me working days, you working nights, our living on opposite sides of town?"

"So," she said slowly, not looking at him, "you think we should live together. That would solve one problem, but we'd still be working conflicting hours."

He halted in front of the bed and grabbed her hands, squeezing them urgently. "We can work it all out, Aubrey. Maybe you could find a daytime job."

Her stomach began to tighten. Her instincts were telling her to say no, to leave, to preserve her independence, but she fought them, determined to give Robert's suggestion a chance. "I could get another job," she said, her voice low. "And with Maggie moving out there's certainly plenty of room."

"Plenty of—I assumed we'd live here. My apartment's big enough, and I really don't want to share my home with another couple."

She stared at him, her eyes wide. He wanted her to quit her job, leave her apartment. The fear that she had been fighting the past few minutes, the past few weeks, overwhelmed her. She couldn't give up everything for Robert and make herself dependent on him. She needed her escape routes!

"No!" she cried, leaping off the bed. "I knew you would try to do this," she accused him. "I knew it after our first date. You want to rearrange my life. How come? Did a few too many people at that party raise their brows at your West Side bartending girlfriend? Don't I fit into your life easily enough? Or is it just that you need to feel in control, need to take away my independence? Well, forget it, Browning!"

She strode down the hall to the apartment door. As she flung it open she turned for one final remark, and almost fell when she discovered Robert standing not two inches from her. For a moment, as she gazed into blue eyes that were filled with confusion at her sudden outburst, she softened. Her body, so abruptly deprived of his lovemaking, strained for his touch. What harm would it do to live here with him, a part of her asked. She certainly was no novice at getting new jobs, so that wouldn't be a problem. And his apartment, though small, was very nice.

No. She shook her head. If she gave in once, she might never stop giving in.

"I can't, Robert," she murmured. She stepped out into the hall.

"Aubrey." His voice halted her at the top of the stairs. "Don't just leave. Please. Let's talk about this. Regardless of what I've said, I don't want to rearrange your life."

She took a deep breath but didn't turn to look at him. "I need to think. I need to . . ." She started down the stairs.

"Don't run away! For God's sake, Aubrey, for once in your life, don't run away."

Again she stopped and looked up at him. "I'm not running away," she said, her voice dull and unforgiving. "I'm leaving."

Her steps echoed with mocking lightness as she slowly descended the stairs. From the third floor Robert could hear her open the downstairs door, and flinched when it banged shut. He turned with an aching weariness and walked back into his apartment.

12

SOMETIME DURING THE NIGHT, between sleeping fitfully and restlessly pacing his apartment, Robert decided all was not lost. He had made a mistake. He hadn't been sensitive enough to Aubrey's fears, fears he thought had been conquered. After she had calmed down, in a day or two, he'd talk to her, tell her he wanted to marry her. Maybe that would scare her off forever, but he had to be honest with Aubrey.

He decided to give her until five o'clock on Sunday afternoon, and if he hadn't heard from her by then, he'd track her down. Saturday passed peculiarly, some hours speeding by as he cleaned his apartment, shopped for groceries, ran into a friend on the street and stopped to have a drink with him. Other hours, however, dragged unbearably, when he had nothing to do and his thoughts turned inevitably to Aubrey. Where was she, he'd wonder. What was she doing? How was she feeling? Was she missing him yet?

When Saturday night finally arrived, he was overwhelmingly tempted to go to Alex's, to seek her out there and force her to listen to him while she was trapped behind the bar. Desperate for anything else to occupy his mind, he finally decided to go to a movie. He hated going to movies alone, but at least his attention would be captured for two hours.

He didn't consider the oddness of being a man alone in New York City on a Saturday night until he was standing in the movie line. As he looked around, it seemed he was the only single person in the entire crowd. Everyone else appeared to be with someone, from the elderly couples to the groups of giggling high-school girls. And of course there were the younger couples, the men and women standing close to each other, holding hands, talking intently or just gazing into each other's eyes. Robert felt a potent, aching loneliness, worse than any loneliness he'd ever felt. Was this what it would be like if he lost Aubrey forever? What if he already had? How would he survive?

Again he was tempted to bolt for the nearest cab and head directly for Alex's. He would drag Aubrey out from behind the bar and carry her off. He couldn't, though. His logic reasserted itself, told him that Aubrey—not to mention Alex—wouldn't allow herself to be kidnapped at eight o'clock on a Saturday night. Besides, he had no place to take her. His apartment, after last night, was definitely out, and there was something too sleazy about checking into a hotel for only one night without any luggage.

The line began moving then, filing into the theater, and Robert followed along. He hoped it would be a good movie.

SUNDAY WASN'T MUCH BETTER. Robert tried to lose himself in the massive *New York Times*, but his attention kept wandering. It was a gloomy day, the sky dark with rain clouds, the air heavy with humidity. Not a day to inspire him to go outside, so he prowled around his apartment, occasionally glancing at the Yankees baseball game on television, occasionally glaring at the phone—which rang twice: his mother and a wrong number. More often he stared at the clock, willing it to move more quickly. Perversely, it seemed to move more slowly, but finally it was five o'clock. Aubrey was supposed to work this Sunday: still, he dialed her home number first. The phone rang once, twice. Then he heard a clicking sound and finally her voice.

"Hi. This is Aubrey at 555-1729. I can't come to the phone right now. If you leave your name, number and a message after the tone, I'll get back to you just as soon as I can. Talk to you soon. Bye."

He held on to the phone until he heard the tone, then hung up. He didn't want to leave a message; he wanted to talk to the woman herself. He dialed Alex's.

"Hello, Alex's," a man's voice said.

"Hello," Robert said. "Is Aubrey Jones there?"

"Uh, no," the man said, faltering a bit. "No, she's not here today. Uh, you want to leave a message?"

"No. Thanks." Robert hung up.

"Damn," he said softly, and the word seemed to bounce off the walls of the silent apartment. Where was she? Was she not answering her phone, just listening to the messages to see who was calling, then deciding whether or not to pick up the receiver? Or was she at Alex's, having told everybody she wasn't in to anyone who called?

He dialed her number again, waited out her message, then said, "Aubrey, it's Robert. I'm sorry. Please call me. We need to talk." He held on to the phone until he heard his time run out on the machine, then hung up.

If she was there and listening, she obviously wasn't ready to talk.

He called Alex's again; this time a woman answered the phone.

"I'd like to leave a message for Aubrey Jones," he said.

"Leave a message?" she repeated, perplexed. "But— Oh. Oh, yeah. A message for Aubrey. Okay, go ahead."

She was there, Robert thought. He was sure of it. Should he go over there right now? No. They wouldn't be able to talk while she was working, and it would be difficult for both of them to be in the same room now and not be able to talk. He'd just leave the message.

"Tell her that Robert Browning called, that I'm sorry and that I need to talk to her right away."

"Robert Browning," the woman said slowly, as if she was writing it down. "Hey, you gonna marry a woman named Elizabeth Barrett?"

Robert rolled his eyes. "Not if I can help it," he muttered.

"Sorry. I guess you get those kind of comments a lot. Let's see," she went on. "Robert Browning called, he's sorry and please call ASAP."

"Right. Thanks very much."

"Sure thing. Bye."

"Bye."

He made himself a hamburger for dinner and ate it while watching *60 Minutes*. He forced himself not to think about the phone that wasn't ringing. After he'd cleaned up his kitchen, he stretched out on the couch with a science-fiction book he'd borrowed from Aubrey. It was a good book but not good enough, for he found his thoughts drifting inexorably to Aubrey. He remembered when they'd first met, how enchanted he'd been by her. He remembered their first date, their first kiss. The wonderful look of shock on her face when he'd told her he was going to kidnap her. Her on the beach, her wild hair blowing in the wind, her face turned to the sun. And in the early-morning light, her eyes soft with sleep and love, her body naked and warm and enticing, pressed close to his beneath the blankets.

"Oh, God." Robert dropped the book on the floor and viciously rubbed his eyes. "Stop thinking about her. You'll drive yourself crazy."

He turned on his own answering machine, grabbed his wallet and keys and stormed out of the apartment. In five minutes he was at his health club—which fortunately stayed open twenty-four hours—and in another ten minutes he was in the pool, racing from one end to the other in a savage crawl stroke. When he climbed out of the pool forty-five minutes later, the only things on his mind, thankfully, were a hot shower to ease the painful exhaustion in his arms and legs and a soft bed in which he could sleep for a long, long time.

"HI. THIS IS Aubrey at 55—"

"Damn!" Robert exclaimed, and dropped the receiver into its cradle as if it had burned him.

Friday afternoon, and still he hadn't been able to find Aubrey. She had just disappeared, with the help of her friends. When he'd returned home from the health club last Sunday night, there had been no message on his machine. Likewise Monday night.

Knowing she worked that night, he went over to Alex's. She wasn't there, and when he asked Alex where she was, the man just shrugged and said she'd called in sick. Remembering Alex's subtle warning the first night he had come to the bar to meet Aubrey, Robert decided not to press the issue and left.

He walked up to Aubrey's apartment building and called her from a phone booth on the corner. He got the answering machine. When he went to the door of the building, Hal, the doorman, met him with a woeful expression on his face.

"I'm sorry, Mr. Browning," he said, with all the dignity and firmness of a Park Avenue doorman who was guarding a Rockefeller or a Vanderbilt. "I'm not allowed to let you in."

"Not allowed! What do you mean?"

"Ms Jones gave me very explicit instructions. I was not to allow Robert Browning to enter the building."

The frustration of the past three days was building in Robert, and he was tempted to push Hal aside and charge into the apartment. But he knew, even if he were at her door, chances were slim that Aubrey would see him; all he'd get for his efforts would be charges laid against him. He could see the newspaper headline now: East Side Lawyer Arrested for Assaulting West Side Doorman in Attempt to See Bartender Girlfriend.

On Tuesday he tried a different tactic. He sent flowers, balloons and more flowers at intervals throughout the day. The message on the first card was "I'm sorry"; on the second, "I miss you"; on the third, "I love you."

By Wednesday he was frantic, and decided to try a sneak attack. He called Maggie and was amazed when he got hold of her on his first try.

"Maggie, this is Robert Browning," he said cautiously when she answered the phone.

"Well, well, well," she said. "Isn't this a surprise."

"Oh, no," he groaned. "Not you, too."

"You were supposed to open up to her, Robert, not consume her."

"Look, I handled it badly. I've never proposed to anyone before. Why won't she at least talk to me?"

"Just so that you can tell her you want her to change her entire life for you?"

"Have a heart, Maggie. I want to see her. I *need* to see her. Can't you help me?"

There was a long silence; then Maggie sighed. "There's not much I can do, Robert. Honest. I don't think she's avoiding you because she doesn't want to see you at all, but because she needs the time to think, to figure a few things out. She's not *ready* to see you yet."

He managed to bite back a rather rude word. "All right. I'll buy that. I don't have much choice."

"Just hang in there for a little bit longer," Maggie said. "It'll work out."

"Easy for you to say," he muttered.

On Thursday he forced himself not to call and tried very hard not to even think about Aubrey. It was difficult, though, when he ran into Harry Benton that afternoon, and Harry asked after Aubrey and suggested that Robert bring her over for dinner sometime.

That Friday afternoon he gave it one more try, only to reach, again, her answering machine. He didn't think he could "hang in there for a little bit longer" anymore. He called a woman named Sharon, whom he had dated several times before he met Aubrey. He apologized for calling her on such short notice and asked if she was available for dinner that evening. She laughed and said, "Give me two minutes and I will be."

They ate in Little Italy on the Lower East Side, as far away from the Upper West Side as Robert could get. He realized with some guilt that he wasn't a very good dinner companion, but Sharon seemed to understand and kept the conversation light and inconsequential. Afterward they walked up through SoHo, enjoying the pleasant evening and the comparative quiet of that section of town.

They hadn't walked far when they came upon a young man sitting on the sidewalk, his back against the wall of an abandoned warehouse, several paintings propped up beside him. Robert glanced quickly at the paintings and kept walking, then stopped and turned back.

The painting closest to the artist was small and delicate and exquisite, very different from the others. It depicted a man, tall and muscular, his head and arms thrown back, his naked body taut and tense. Wrapping vaguely about him was a silvery mist. The mist was not natural, though, for the longer Robert looked, the more he could see that the tendrils of the mist were like arms and fingers clutching the man. A woman's hair fanned out behind him, while her face, hinted at in the most fascinating way, pressed close to his side. The man, Robert decided, was in the grip of love.

He gestured to the painting. "How much?" he asked.

FOR SEVERAL MINUTES Aubrey stared without moving at the painting clutched in her hands. Marcus was on duty as doorman that night. He had buzzed her at a little past eleven to tell her there was a package for her downstairs. Robert Browning had dropped it off, he added. She had gone downstairs, not sure what she was feeling most: relief, trepidation or simple curiosity. Her curiosity had now been satisfied, but the relief and trepidation were still battling it out.

Robert had attached a note, a brief one, to the brown paper bag the painting had been wrapped in. It said, "The artist titled this painting *Nighttime*. I call it *Love*."

She was fairly certain she understood what he meant. She recognized the fog that surrounded the man in the painting as a female entity. Judging from the expression on the man's face, he could be either in agony or ecstasy. The more she thought about it, the more she feared Robert had interpreted it as agony.

But, she argued with herself, why make a gift of an original painting that could have cost him as much as two hundred dollars, even on the street, if the message was that love was agony and, she assumed, he didn't want to suffer any longer?

"Why is he being so vague?" she asked Merlin, who was curled up beside her on the sofa. "He was always so straightforward before."

She set the painting down on the coffee table and leaned her head back. Unbidden memories of their weeks together flooded her mind. She remembered the laughter and the wariness, his understanding of her hesitation and his frustration with it. And the sexual tension that had continually grown between them, until the night it had exploded and they had shared such rapturous delight. Even the thought of their lovemaking was enough to make her grow weak, to make a honeyed warmth flow through her and a throbbing heaviness begin in her lower body.

"Oh, Merlin," she whispered, her voice cracking with sorrow, "what am I going to do? I love him, but I'm so scared."

She got up, walked to the French doors and gazed out at the brightly lit city. She thought of their first dinner, when they had sat in her bedroom and looked out on the night. She had told him that she thought there was magic out there, magic that was just waiting to happen to her. And it had happened. Why was she rejecting it?

She had been frightened last Friday night, frightened by his proposal and her own declaration of love. She had realized by Sunday that Robert hadn't meant to hurt her, to run roughshod over her sensibilities when he had suggested that she give up her job, when he had assumed they would live in his apartment. Her love had urged her to make up with him, to forgive him and try to compromise. Something, however, held her back.

Suddenly restless, filled with the need to get out, she whirled and in two steps was at her phone. She quickly dialed a number. The phone was picked up on the second ring.

"Hello, Ted?" she said. "This is Aubrey. Did I wake you?"

"No. Five minutes later, though, and you would have."

"Sorry about that. Do you suppose I could borrow William Butler for a little while? I have the sudden urge to take a walk. I could keep him here overnight, so I wouldn't have to wake you when I brought him back."

"Fine. Come on down."

Aubrey hung up the phone and quickly grabbed some money, her driver's license—for identification in case of some mishap—keys and a lightweight jacket. In less than a minute she was knocking on Ted and Bruce's door.

Ted opened it immediately, holding a dog leash in one hand. On the other end of the leash was a pure white dog whose head came to about Ted's hip.

"Here you go, P.T.," Ted said. "You can try knocking on the door when you get back, and if we don't answer, just take him upstairs."

"No problem. Thanks, Ted." She took the leash from him. "Come on, William Butler."

The Irish wolfhound obediently followed her out of the apartment, obviously excited by the prospect of a midnight walk. Once outside, the dog headed instantly for Riverside Park, but Aubrey firmly reined him in.

"Dog or no dog," she said to him, "there's no way I'm walking through the park at this time of night. We're going to go where all the people are."

They walked the two blocks east to Broadway, then turned south. As she had expected, Broadway was filled with people. Not as many as during the day, certainly, but still an amazing number. There were the young girls in short skirts and bright tops with bands of lace or tulle in their hair. There were the boys, who didn't look much different in their leather jackets and tight jeans than they had when Aubrey had been in high school. There were a few street people, standing on the corners, looking lost. Mostly there were men and women in their twenties and thirties, dressed in summer casual wear, pastels and white. The couples had their arms around each other, and the open affection on many faces made Aubrey's heart ache.

That could be me and Robert, she thought. Instead she was walking with William Butler. A handsome, dignified escort, to be sure, but not someone who could hold her when she was sad, exchange joyous kisses with her when she was happy or join her in ecstasy when she was in the mood for love.

"Or when *he* was in the mood for love," she muttered.

She continued walking, pausing only when William Butler had to check out an interesting smell at a parking meter or at one of the all-night Korean fruit stands. She didn't realize how far she'd gone until she was stopped by a long red light and finally looked up at the street sign.

"Seventy-ninth?" she murmured in disbelief. "That's quite a ways from home, William Butler."

Sitting contentedly beside her, William Butler wagged his tail and gave a short bark.

Aubrey looked east up Seventy-ninth Street, east to Central Park; beyond that was the Upper East Side. Where Robert lived. He suddenly seemed so close, just a short bus ride away. She was filled with the overpowering need to see him, and her fear instantly fought that need.

With shocking clarity Aubrey realized how wrong she had been. She'd been wrong when she had told Robert she trusted him. She hadn't. Though she loved him, she had still expected him to hurt her, to take her love then abandon her. She didn't think his intention had been to rearrange her life last Friday night, but she had used his words as an excuse to give in to her fear, to run away as if the hounds of hell were after her.

Hell was where she had been all this week. She'd been miserable every time she refused to answer his calls, on the verge of tears every time she heard his voice on her answering machine. She remembered the flowers and balloons he'd sent her and their accompanying messages: "I'm sorry, I miss you, I love you." She thought of the painting he'd given her, of the man enfolded by the misty woman. What more did Robert have to do to prove his love, to gain her trust?

"That's it, William Butler," she said to the dog. "I don't want to be miserable anymore. That man loves me, and if I can't give him my own love wholeheartedly, I *deserve* to be miserable."

She looked down at the dog. "The immediate worry right now is finding a cab driver who'll take us over to the East Side."

Luck was with them. The first cab that stopped at her hail was an old Checker, which could easily sit five people in the back. With her most charming smile, Aubrey asked if the driver would be willing to take her and her dog to the East Side. She assured him that William Butler was not vicious and was well trained, and the driver assured her that it was no problem for such a lovely lady.

When the cab dropped them off in front of Robert's building, Aubrey tried to calm her racing heart. She had little success. Her decision had been impulsive, and she hadn't considered that Robert might not be home. Or worse, that he might not be alone.

"He'd better be here, William Butler," she said, unconsciously tightening her hold on the dog's leash, "'cause all we've got left to get home is fifty cents."

Taking a deep breath and trying to blank out her rampaging fears and second thoughts, she marched up the steps and rang Robert's bell.

Three long rings later she was rewarded.

"Yes?" came Robert's voice out of the intercom.

He sounded only a little irritated. "It's me, Robert. Aubrey."

There was a long pause, then, "Aubrey?"

Definitely not irritated, she thought, but certainly puzzled. "Yes. Can I come up?"

"What are you doing out on the streets in the middle of the night?" his voice boomed.

Uh-oh, she thought. They'd skipped irritation and gone directly to anger.

"I'm well protected. Can I come up?"

"What? Oh, yes. Of course you can come up."

The downstairs buzzer sounded, and Aubrey quickly pushed the door open. She ushered William Butler in, turned to make sure no one was following her, then closed the door.

Robert was waiting when she reached the third floor. She had apparently gotten him out of bed, for he was wearing a blue robe and white pajama bottoms. He also looked tired, with stubble shadowing his jaw and dark circles shadowing his eyes. And the look in those eyes wasn't encouraging. He looked wary at best.

The wariness abruptly changed to surprise when she reached the landing, William Butler beside her.

"Who's that?" Robert asked, staring at the dog.

"William Butler. He belongs to Ted and Bruce. You remember them, don't you?"

Robert closed his eyes briefly and nodded. He muttered something that could have been, "How could I forget?" Aubrey decided not to ask him to repeat himself.

"Come on in," he said, standing back from the open doorway. "I presume William Butler is housebroken."

"Don't be insulting," she said, striving for a light tone. "William Butler is much too dignified to be anything else."

"Of course," Robert murmured.

Once inside the apartment, Aubrey unleashed the dog. "You don't mind if he takes a look around, do you? He likes exploring new places."

Robert glanced quickly down the hall, toward the bedroom. "No," he said. "I don't mind."

Aubrey cast her own suspicious glance down the hall. "I'm not interrupting anything, am I?" she asked, her voice small and timid despite her best intentions. Why, oh, why had she come, she asked herself. Couldn't she have waited for a more normal time, or at least phoned first?

He smiled gently, as if sensing her sudden qualms. "No, you're not interrupting anything. There's just a plate of crackers and cheese on my bed, that's all."

"Crackers and—Oh, no!" She took off down the hall and dashed into the bedroom, just in time to see William Butler sink his sharp white teeth into the wedge of cheese. "Oh, William Butler!" she cried. "You know that's not good for your digestive system."

She deftly snatched the rest of the cheese from him and turned to find Robert watching her. He was leaning against the doorjamb, one leg crossed in front of the other, his hands stuffed into the pockets of his robe.

"I'm sorry, Robert," she said. "He's got this thing about cheese."

The dog whined at her side, and she looked down into his soulful, appealing eyes. She shook her head. "Forget it, kid. If Ted and Bruce found out, they'd never let me play with you again."

Robert chuckled and took the cheese from her. "I think I'll dispose of this," he said, and started back down the hall. William Butler walked beside him, looking hopefully at the cheese. Aubrey followed. As Robert and William Butler disappeared into the kitchen, she halted in the living room.

What a disaster. What had possessed her to arrive at Robert's at one o'clock in the morning with a miniature horse? If she had intended to convince him that she did, indeed, love and trust him, she was going about it in a peculiar way. But she was here now and might as well make the best of it. Taking a deep breath, she walked into the kitchen. Robert was leaning back against the sink, watching as William Butler eagerly 'apped up water from a large bowl.

"Good idea," she said, gesturing to the dog. "He was probably thirsty from that long walk."

She turned away and pretended to study with great interest an empty wine bottle sitting on a counter. Actually, she was trying not to look at Robert. His robe had fallen open slightly, revealing his naked chest and the enticing hair covering it. His pose was so casual and tempting that she could just imagine walking into his arms, leaning against his solid, long body, becoming enveloped by his warmth, his love.

Disconcerted by her thoughts, her longings, she picked up the wine bottle and turned it over and over in her hands. The silence was oppressive, and she shot a quick glance at Robert. He was looking at her, all wariness gone from his eyes and a tender smile on his lips.

"You know," he said quietly, "this all reminds me of the night we met."

"Oh?" she said. That wasn't quite what she'd expected him to say.

"If it hadn't been for Merlin and your impulsiveness, we would never have met." He straightened away from the sink and took a step closer to her. "You took my breath away that night, so natural and open and trusting—toward me, at least. Anyone else looking at your life would find it confusing, maddening, but you accept it. It's perfectly natural to you that a dozen people would help you look for your cat—" another step toward her "—or that a complete stranger would guard that cat in a deserted parking lot—" another step "—or that there's magic in the stars."

She looked down, looked away, then finally looked up into his eyes. He cupped her face in his hands, his fingers inching into her thick hair while his thumbs gently traced her cheekbones.

"I love you," he whispered. "You made me angry, hurt me when you never returned any of my messages all week, but I love you. I probably always will."

Tears filled her eyes. He still loved her. Oh, thank heavens.

"I put it very badly last week," he went on, staring into her eyes. "I didn't mean to try to take over your life. I was just so afraid I might lose you, afraid to ask for too much or too little."

"What do you want?" she asked, her voice quavering. "What do you want from me?"

He dropped a kiss on her lips. "I want to marry you. I want to live with you anywhere you want to live. All I ask is to be with you forever—with you and our children."

"Ch-children?"

He nodded. "Children."

"Oh, Robert." She flung her arms around him and hugged him tightly. "I love you. I love you so much, and I'm so sorry I hurt you this week, but I was scared, too, scared I might be wrong, that somehow all of this was wrong."

He tilted her head up. "How could this be wrong? We have magic on our side."

She laughed, even as the tears started flowing. They hugged each other, swaying slightly, not speaking. After a few minutes Robert moved back and looked down at her.

"Will you marry me?" he asked seriously.

She nodded. "Yes."

"No doubts, hesitations, fears about not being able to commit yourself?"

"They may crop up every now and again, but you've eased so many of those fears, showing me how to trust, both in myself and in another person." She laughed slightly. "I don't know if I'll ever find a steady job and stick with it for thirty years, but I've now been with Alex longer than I've been anywhere else, and that seems like a good sign."

"You could try painting again," he suggested, "since you wouldn't have to worry about where your next meal's coming from."

"There's a thought." She eased out of his arms. The feel of his body, so scantily clad, against her own deprived body, was proving too much for her. She figured they either needed to continue this conversation in the living room or stop talking altogether. She started for the living room.

"Oh, by the way," she added as she walked, "did I tell you the Sullivans are moving out? They've decided they don't want to raise a child in the city, and since Mitch has been offered a job teaching at some small midwestern college, they're leaving. Next month."

She was about to sit down on the sofa when she was swept off her feet. Robert's mouth stopped her startled exclamation.

"Does this mean you're going to be all alone in that big apartment?" he asked.

"Uh-huh."

"Need a new roommate?"

"Why? You thinking of applying?"

His lips settled firmly on hers, and he kissed her with such fervency and love that she could do little more than cling to him.

"Yes, I'm applying," he said when he released her.

"Applying for what?" she asked dreamily.

"You'll see," he said, and carried her down the hall to the bedroom.

ATTRACTIVE, SPACE SAVING BOOK RACK

Display your most prized novels on this handsome and sturdy book rack. The hand-rubbed walnut finish will blend into your library decor with quiet elegance, providing a practical organizer for your favorite hard-or soft-covered books.

Only $9.95

Approximately 16" x 8" when assembled

Assembles in seconds!

To order, rush your name, address and zip code, along with a check or money order for $10.70 ($9.95 plus 75¢ postage and handling) (New York residents add appropriate sales tax), payable to *Silhouette Reader Service* to:

In the U.S.

Silhouette Reader Service
Book Rack Offer
901 Fuhrmann Blvd.
P.O. Box 1325
Buffalo, NY 14269-1325

Offer not available in Canada.

BKR-2